PLAIN TALES OF THE AFGHAN BORDER

BY THE SAME AUTHOR

Verse: Grim and Gay
Poems from the Persian
The Golden Pomegranate
A new Selection from the Rubaiyat of Omar Khayyam
Poems
Translation or Travesty?
(*An Enquiry into Robert Graves's version of some Rubaiyat of Omar Khayyam*)
Oriental Proverbs

PLAIN TALES OF THE AFGHAN BORDER

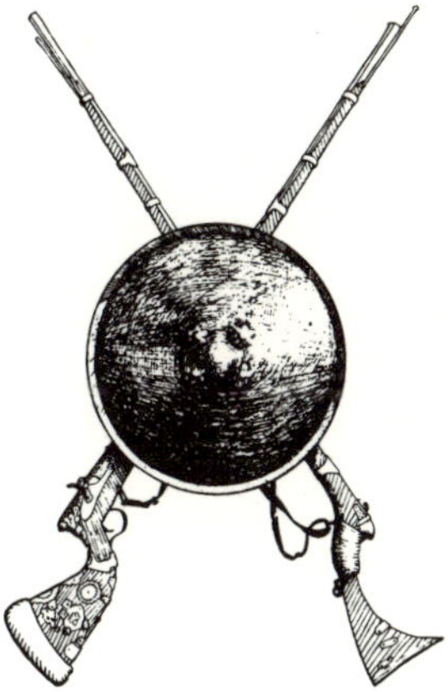

John Charles Edward Bowen

LONDON
SPRINGWOOD BOOKS

First published 1982 by Springwood Books Ltd
22 Chewter Lane, Windlesham, Surrey

ISBN 0 86254 102 6

Set in 12 on 13 pt Bembo
Printed and bound in Great Britain at
The Camelot Press Ltd, Southampton

We who with songs beguile your pilgrimage
And swear that Beauty lives though lilies die,
We Poets of the proud old lineage
Who sing to find your hearts, we know not why, –
What shall we tell you? Tales, marvellous tales . . .

JAMES ELROY FLECKER
The Golden Journey to Samarkand

TO

MOHAMMAD ZARIF KHAN

PRINCE OF STORY-TELLERS

Acknowledgements

Acknowledgements are due to the Editors of *The Contemporary Review* and *The Journal of the Royal Asiatic Society*, in which 'The Diplomacy of High Asia' and 'The Story of the Blind Man of Taxila' have already been published.

The design of two jezails, one from Waziristan and the other from Baluchistan, printed on the jacket and title page of this book and all the other decorations, except the one on page 12 were drawn by the author for the original edition of *The Golden Pomegranate*, published in 1957 by Thacker & Co., Bombay.

Contents

Introduction

Anyone who has read *The Golden Pomegranate* will have already met Mohammad Zarif Khan, for it was he who, during the course of a journey through Tribal Territory to meet a jirga of the Tilliwal Sayyeds, introduced me to the poetry of the greatest of the Pushtu Poets, Khushhal Khan Khatak. When, soon after, I composed an English verse translation of 'The Lasses of the Adam Khel', I had no premonition that, during the coming months, Zarif would provide the keyhole through which I would be able to look into the enchanted world of Pushtu story-telling. But that, I am glad to say, is exactly what happened.

Early in the autumn of 1943, as soon as the formalities of taking over the Mansehra Sub-Division had been completed, I set out to beat the bounds of my parish. The first place I visited was Oghi, a village twenty miles away on the other side of a mountain pass, whose Fort confronts the looming mass of the Black Mountain, which lies in Tribal Territory, only a short distance beyond the demarcated frontier.

I was met there by Mohammad Zarif Khan who, as Political Tehsildar, Oghi, was in charge of the day-to-day administration of that stretch of the frontier. Mohammad Zarif was a tall robust man of about the same age as myself, whose pleasant face, which tended to crinkle into smiles, indicated that he found life not only enjoyable but often immensely amusing. He was a scion of the leading Tirah family of Kuki Khel Afridis, and had been educated at the Islamia College, Peshawar, before entering the Provincial Civil Service, the highest rank of which he later adorned.

That first official tour was the pattern of all my subsequent visits to Oghi. When the administrative problems had been discussed and settled, and the files I had brought with me from Mansehra had been annotated and put away, Zarif and I would repair to the bare living-room of the Resthouse under the wall of the Fort to have supper together. Afterwards, in spring, summer, and autumn we used to sit talking outside under the stars, but in winter we would pull our chairs close to a blazing log fire, to beguile with amicable conversation the lonely tedium of the night.

After several visits to Oghi had passed in this pleasant fashion, I began to realize that on each occasion Mohammad Zarif had told me at least one memorable story – either an account of some exciting adventure in which he himself figured as its unassuming hero, or an anecdote illustrating the part his own family had played in the history of Afghanistan, or one of the humorous or near-tragic stories about everyday life in Tirah, the famous tract of mountainous tribal territory to the west of Peshawar, where his boyhood had been spent.

When I realized the importance of my discovery, I consulted Zarif how a permanent record of his stories could best be made, and we decided that in future whenever I visited Oghi I would bring with me a supply of rough paper* on which to write down in longhand the stories as he related them to me. That is how it happened that, the next time I visited Oghi, Zarif and I found ourselves sitting down again after supper at the bare Resthouse table, I with a pencil poised, and Zarif opposite to me, his eyes sparkling with the pleasure of a born story-teller about to launch into the narration of an enthralling tale.

Zarif would then commence, simply and directly, with words such as those that introduce 'The Tale of the Emir's Sword': *It happened during the latter part of the nineteenth century . . . that the Emir of Afghanistan sent a summons to the jirga of the Kuki Khel Afridis . . .* Thereafter the story would unfold, with all its tensions and

* The buff vernacular Court Order forms, on the back of which I recorded Zarif's stories, are now in the India Office Library.

fascinating circumstantial detail until the denouement is reached, and the moral (if the story happens to have one) is summed up, either in a Pushtu proverb or in a quotation from a famous Persian poet.

When several months had passed, during which I had on successive visits to Oghi written down Zarif's stories in his own words, I began to consider how I could share with other people the pleasure the stories gave me by having them published as a book. The first difficulty that I saw would have to be overcome was that Zarif and I were both serving officers, and it would therefore be essential that certain recent incidents described in the stories, as well as the identity of any officials who figured in them, should be disguised. It was of course impossible for me to foresee, and was indeed unthinkable when I transcribed the stories, that the Indian Empire, to the service of which the lives of Zarif and myself were then dedicated, would cease to exist a mere three years later when, on 15th August, 1947, independence would be granted to the newly-established governments of India and Pakistan.

On that date it became no longer possible for Zarif's administrative indiscretions, and my approval implicit in the way I recorded them, to become the subject of departmental enquiry and punishment. Instead it suddenly seemed possible that the account I would one day write of how Zarif thought and acted while serving the Raj immediately on the other side of the historic watershed of the handover of power in India, would show how well the Raj was served by a member of one of the proud races it governed – by indeed an Afridi official who sometimes acted ruthlessly, and often unconventionally, but always with an imaginative strength of purpose that carried all before it.

One of the senior officers who, I realized at the time, would have to remain anonymous was Lt.-Col. (later Sir Rupert) Hay, who was the Political Agent in Waziristan who reprimanded Zarif for arranging (at great personal risk) the execution in tribal territory of the dangerous criminal, Jamuri. Because Colonel Hay's words,

'It was nothing but a bloody assassination', were an essential part of the story, I suggested to Zarif as he was relating it that, in addition to omitting the name of the P.A., we had better ensure that the background also of the story should be unrecognizable. That is why, although the story of 'The Death of an Outlaw' is authentic in every detail, neither I nor anyone else can now tell what the names of Gul Tangi Fort and the Koh-i-Ashkar mountains really are.

Similarly, but for reasons of loyalty rather than any concern for the consequences, I have in 'The Diplomacy of High Asia' changed the name of my predecessor as Assistant Commissioner, Mansehra (whose dealings with the Kohistani jirga were a dismal failure, whereas the diplomacy of his subordinate, Zarif, achieved dazzling success) to 'Toby O'Brien'. Both these names are dear to me because they are those of my godfather, Lt.-Col. 'Toby' O'Brien, who was himself an officer in the illustrious 'Foreign and Political Department of the Government of India' at the time when, on 25th October, 1909, I became his godchild in the little church of All Saints on Malabar Hill, Bombay.

It had been my hope in the beginning that if it ever proved possible for Zarif's stories to be published, they should be expressed as far as possible in his own words. But when, two years ago, I took the MS. out of the *yakdan* in which it had reposed during the previous thirty-five years, it was clear that a number of alterations would have to be made. This was largely because, when Zarif told me the stories, I understood as well as he did exactly what he was talking about, whereas most people today, if they could read the stories just as he told them to me, would not. When, for example, in the story of 'The Versatility of Amir Khan Afridi', Zarif mentioned the town of Baramula, I knew (because the main road to Srinager, by which I have often travelled, passes through it) that it is 'a small town of wooden houses interspersed with poplar trees, which stands at the edge of the mountain-encircled Wular Lake'. I therefore added this brief description, because it is unlikely that a European reader of the story would today know anything about this or indeed any other village in the Vale of Kashmir.

I had a different reason for altering the incident in 'The Story of the Blind Man of Taxila', when the Blind Man insisted that the princess should walk over the roof of the pavilion in the king's garden. It seemed essential to specify that the pavilion was constructed of *wood* because the Blind Man could not possibly have heard the rhythm of the princess's footsteps passing overhead if the roof had been constructed of marble, which is the material ordinarily used in India for such a building.

The final tale, 'The Conundrum of the Three Suitors of the Princess of Baghdad', was the last story Zarif told me before my wife and I left the North-West Frontier in April 1945 on transfer to the Persian Gulf. I had much official business to transact at Mansehra on the day when Zarif came to see me to say goodbye, and there remained only a very short time in which to jot down the bare outline of the story. Since it was a tale in the tradition of the Arabian Nights, and not the account of an historical event, I have felt at liberty to tell the story entirely in my own words, embroidering it where necessary.

To me the most deeply interesting of all Zarif's stories was that of 'The Blind Man of Taxila', which was published in the November 1980 issue of the *Journal of the Royal Asiatic Society*. When, early in 1980, I offered the story to the learned Editor of the *Journal*, and explained its background and provenance, he started by being suspicious of its authenticity, and later confessed that he suspected it of being an elaborate hoax. Zarif and I have been the gainers from these (I still think unworthy) suspicions because it caused the Royal Society to bring their most searching scrutiny to bear on our little story, with the result that it passed muster with flying colours, not only with the Publications Committee, whose job is to advise the Editor, but also with the Specialist Referee, to whom it was deemed necessary to submit it for the final clearance.

The 'clean bill of health', awarded to our light-hearted deviation from the usual portentous gravity of the contents of the Royal Asiatic Society's *Journal*, was printed immediately after the story when it appeared in the 1980 issue. It runs as follows:

> 'An extensive search in the standard sources on the folklore of India, and of the North-West Frontier, has produced no close parallel for the tale reported here. In spite of the Muslim tribal milieu from which it comes, it is obvious that the story reflects in the main the older background, and attitudes, of a pre-Muslim Hindu society, with its emphasis on considerations of caste. The name of the ruler featured, "Chandradev", suggests that any historical allusion intended is to a king named Candragupta: presumably, therefore, to Candragupta Maurya (reigned 317–293 B.C.) who was in fact a younger, not an older, contemporary of Alexander the Great, as the story claims. Such a small chronological error would hardly be unusual in oral transmission. Historical writers who draw on various Indian traditions have often stated that Candragupta Maurya began his career at Taxila, that he was of Vaisya descent (Romila Thapar, *Asoka and the Decline of the Mauryas*, Oxford, 1961, 13), or of illegitimate birth (V. A. Smith, *Early History of India*, Oxford, 1914, 117). Editor.'

I feel deeply grateful for this verdict, which confers on the simple folk tale, told to me by Zarif three decades ago, a lifespan of nearly twenty-three centuries. *Bismillah al-rahman al-rahim!*

Petersfield, Hampshire,
June 1981

Pushtu Poetry

A book such as this, which may perhaps be considered to throw fresh light on the way Pathans think, feel, and act, would be incomplete without the inclusion of some of their poetry. During 1944, while I was serving on the Frontier, I translated into English verse the three poems which follow. One was composed by the mighty seventeenth-century Frontier Bard, Khushhal Khan Khatak, one by a distinguished modern Pushtu poet, Sayed Rasul Rasa, and one is a traditional poem expressing the sorrow of ultimate farewell.

Khushhal Khan Khatak is just such a brave, honourable, and romantic leader of a Highland people as Sir Walter Scott might well have honoured with his pen; and he is too diversely interesting as a man, and too famous as a poet throughout the Pushtu-speaking territories of the North-West Frontier and Afghanistan, for me to think of banishing him to the obscurity of a note at the end of this book. Here, instead, is the brief biography of him which I wrote in July 1947, while serving at the Residency, Lahore, as it appears in *The Golden Pomegranate: A selection from the poetry of the Mogul Empire in India 1526–1858*.*

* First published by Thacker & Co., with coloured illustrations by Balai Das, Bombay, 1957. Republished in an edition uniform with *Poems from the Persian* by John Baker, London, 1966.

Khushhal Khan Khatak

A.D. 1613–1690

Khushhal Khan succeeded to the chieftainship of the Khatak tribe in 1641. In accordance with the wise and temperate policy of Shah Jahan he was confirmed in his fief and made responsible for the security of the great highway to Kabul, which runs through Khatak territory between Attock and Peshawar. This policy was reversed when Shah Jahan's son, the uncompromising zealot Aurangzeb, became Emperor, and Khushhal Khan complains bitterly in one of his poems that

Whereas I was an Eagle or a Falcon in the sight of Shah Jahan,
I am now treated as a Crow or Sparrowhawk by Aurangzeb.

Mutual confidence gave way to distrust, and then to hostility; finally Khushhal Khan was seized and sent as a prisoner to the fortress of Gwalior, where, during an unhappy exile of seven years, he wrote much of his poetry.

Aurangzeb, who was as obstinate as he was unperceptive, did not abate the policy by which he hoped to reduce the Border tribes to submission, with the result that, not long after Khushhal's return to his own country, the Afridi tribes rose in revolt, and in 1672 inflicted at 'Ali Masjid, in the Khyber Pass, a terrible defeat on the army of the Mogul Governor of Afghanistan. The whole border at once rose, and Khushhal Khan, seizing the opportunity to pay off his old score against Aurangzeb, threw in his lot with the Afridis. Several years of guerilla warfare ensued, during which Khushhal

Khan inspired his clansmen no less by his skill and bravery as their leader than by the heart-kindling quality of his patriotic songs. Aurangzeb, after spending two fruitless years at Attock directing operations against the tribes, succeeded in encompassing by cajolery and the liberal expenditure of money what he had failed to achieve by force. One by one the Afridi tribes dropped out of the confederacy, till the Khatak clan under Khushhal Khan were alone left to carry on the fight. In the end, betrayed to the enemy (it is said) by one of his sons, Khushhal Khan gave up the unequal struggle. He consoled himself during the remainder of his life by writing caustic verses about his old enemy Aurangzeb, and the Afridi tribes, whose defection had brought to nothing their common struggle for independence from Mogul rule.

Khushhal Khan was an extremely versatile writer. In addition to satires and stirring patriotic songs, he wrote many poems on outdoor subjects such as hawking, a sport to which he was passionately addicted, as well as love poems, stanzas describing the beauties of Nature, and ethical verses. Of the last sort, it would be difficult to find a line more apposite than

A Governor's word is worth more than twenty witnesses,

or more charming than that which asks

What cares the Ass, or Bullock, whether his load be made of flowers?

The epitaph which he wrote for his own grave exemplifies the spirit of this brave and independent-minded man:

Here lies Khushhal among the lonely hills,
Where dust from the far-scouring Mogul horse
Cannot defile his grave.

The Lasses of the Adam Khel

by

KHUSHHAL KHAN KHATAK

The Lasses of the Adam Khel,
As every lover knows,
Are delicately coloured – like
The petals of a rose;
My Love a snowy partridge is,
Who chooses winter time
To seek among the stony fells
A cloak of silver rime.

My Love, my Bird, remember that
A hawk, when he grows old,
Becomes more subtle in the chase,
His stoop becomes more bold:
Surrender then to me, for though
I seem no longer young,
The fervour of my love will taste
Like honey on your tongue.

Beside the Kabul River

by

SAYED RASUL RASA

Where dark the swirling water sweeps,
With woods on either hand,
A young man sits alone and weeps
Upon the river strand.

He sighs, 'Alas my Love was kind,
Alas, my Love pretended
To keep me constantly in mind –
And thus the matter ended.'

A little wave crept up the sand
And touched the poet's feet:
She said 'You do not understand
Where love and friendship meet:

'For if, though lovely as the rose,
No love for thee she bears,
Thy heart should once more gain repose,
Thine eyes forget their tears;

'But if each hour that passes makes
A tally in Grief's score,
Poor Singer, till thy sad heart breaks,
Weep on for evermore.'

A Pathan Warrior's Farewell

Beloved, on a parchment white
With my heart's blood to thee I write;
My pen a dagger, sharp and clean,
Inlaid with golden damascene,
Which I have used, and not in vain,
To keep my honour free from stain.

Now, when our house its mourning wears,
Do not thyself give way to tears:
Instruct our eldest son that I
Was ever anxious thus to die,
For when Death comes the brave are free –
So in thy dreams remember me.

One

THE STORY OF EMRAN

The Fifteenth Malik

"You will recall," said Mohammad Zarif Khan one spring day, as we were walking together under the willow trees in the little valley which opens southward from the Fort at Oghi, "that my great-grandfather had three sons, each of a different mother. The eldest, Haidar Khan, was somewhat crack-brained, so my great-grandfather's choice fell on his second son, Amin Khan, to succeed him as Khan of the Kuki Khel tribe. My grandfather, Mohammad Zaman Khan, seeing that he had no further hope of becoming Khan, and in order to avoid any clash with his elder brother, decided to move over the border into Afghanistan, and to seek his fortune with Sipah Salar Ghulam Haidar Khan. This Afghan general was at that time engaged in subduing the unruly Shinwari tribe, who dwell on the northern slopes of the Safed Koh, not more than thirty miles from my home in the Rajgul valley. In those days the Shinwaris' main occupation was highway robbery on the road between Peshawar and Jalalabad. Their banditry was practised to such an extent that complaints had reached the ears of the Emir, Abdur Rahman, who directed his most trusted general, Ghulam Haidar Khan, to subjugate the Shinwaris and compel them to follow a more orderly way of life.

"My grandfather met Ghulam Haidar Khan at Jalalabad, where the famous general was making preparations for the campaign against the Shinwaris. At their first meeting Ghulam Haidar recognized the sagacity of my grandfather, who was then a sturdily-built young man of twenty, and immediately invited him to join his staff as an A.D.C. My grandfather served in this capacity throughout the operations against the Shinwaris, and subsequently saw active service as the Sipah Salar's right hand man in a number of other campaigns.

"Many years later, when my gradfather was an old man and I had returned from my schooling at the Islamia College, Peshawar, I expressed the opinion that, without an academic education, no man could expect to succeed in life. My grandfather instantly held up his hand and stopped me, saying, 'Child, you are still raw in your knowledge of the world. There have been men who have succeeded in life without even knowing the alphabet.' I sensed from his words that he had some good tale to tell me, so I said, 'Baba, as I am an educated man, you must not expect me to believe things unless you can prove your assertion by an example from life: dogma has no place in the consideration of an educated man: what is asserted must be proved.' This was the opportunity for which my grandfather had been looking. Inhaling a big breath, he opened his eyes wide in triumph, and commenced to relate in a lively manner the tale of Emran, the Fifteenth Malik.

"'My child,' he said, 'Sipah Salar Ghulam Haidar's campaign against the Shinwaris in which, as you know, I took part, entailed several months' hard fighting before it was brought to a victorious conclusion. Eventually the Shinwaris grew tired of fighting us and sent a Mullah to ask for a truce. The Sipah Salar agreed, provided that, on a given day, all fifteen Maliks of the bribe came and surrendered themselves to him at Kahi Fort. On the appointed day the Afghan troops were drawn up, with their bayonets fixed, in the spacious courtyard of the Fort, where a *shamiana* had been erected and a large carpet spread in preparation for the Durbar. All of us officers on the General's staff were jubilant at the successful conclusion of the campaign, and were looking forward to the spectacle of the fifteen leaders of the bandit confederacy, which had so stoutly opposed us, being brought in under armed guard to hear the words with which we felt sure the Sipah Salar intended to chasten them. When the Sipah Salar had seated himself in his chair under the *shamiana*, he nodded to his staff to be seated, and to the escort to bring forward the Maliks. As the latter reached the edge of the carpet, each Elder took off his shoes, salaamed to the Sipah Salar, and asked permission to be seated on the carpet in front of him. This permission having been accorded, the Durbar was declared open.

"Before the Sipah Salar started his address, which we knew would contain many taunts and witticisms, he took the precaution of counting the Maliks. When he reached the end of his count the Sipah Salar's brow grew dark. 'You rogues,' he suddenly shouted, 'where is the fifteenth Malik? Unless he attends this Durbar no settlement with your tribe can be reached. Not to have come in full jirga merely gives me unnecessary trouble.' At this there was much head-shaking and murmuring among the Maliks. Eventually one of them, whose name was Nasir Khan, spoke up. 'Sipah Salar Sahib,' he said, 'the fifteenth Malik is an incorrigible person called Emran, who does not recognize the benefits of an orderly way of life, and when he heard that we had agreed to come and surrender to you he ran away from us and hid among the Afridis on the other side of the Safed Koh range.'

"On hearing this the Sipah Salar rose in fury from his chair, and ordered that the fourteen Maliks were to be removed from his presence and kept under guard until the fifteenth Malik came in and made his submission. He then sent for the *Sudbashi* commanding the cavalry detachment which was on picquet duty outside the Fort, and instructed him to ride at once with his hundred men to the village of Nassian, where the fifteenth Malik had his home, and to live on the village with all his men and horses until further notice.

"After the cavalry had been quartered on Nassian for a few days the relatives of the fifteenth Malik grew restive at having to provide free rations and fodder for the Afghan army. They therefore departed in a body to interview Emran. Now Emran had taken the precaution of removing with him into exile a flock of sheep and goats, as well as a herd of cattle, and was living very happily in a shepherd's hut among the pine trees which clothe the higher slopes of the Safed Koh. When eventually Emran's relatives came face to face with him there, they complained bitterly of the hardships to which they had been subjected by the Sipah Salar since he had absconded, and begged him to return with them and present himself to the Sipah Salar with the other fourteen Maliks of the tribe. When Emran enquired what hardships they had suffered, his kinsmen replied indignantly that everything edible in the village had been seized by the Afghan cavalry, and that they were now hard put to find anything at all to eat. Emran replied very coolly that they should not worry themselves about such petty matters. 'Let the Afghans,' he said, 'eat anything they can find in the village, and when they have consumed everything they will go away. You can then come and live with me here,' he said, 'and help me look after my flocks.' His kinsmen were so enraged with Emran at this heartless reply that they would certainly have seized him, and carried him away captive, if they had not feared the Afridis among whom he had taken refuge. Realizing, however, that nothing would persuade Emran to return with them, they retraced their steps in great despondence to Nassian.

"As Emran had predicted, the Afghan cavalry, after exhausting all the stocks of wheat and hay at Nassian, returned to Kahi Fort, where the Sudbashi reported to the Sipah Salar that there was nothing left for man or beast to eat at Emran's village.

"The Sipah Salar had meanwhile received an urgent message from the Emir that, because there was trouble brewing in Herat, he must wind up the Shinwaris' affairs, and return with all possible despatch to Kabul. Now it so happened that the Afridis, with whom Emran had taken refuge, were men of my own tribe, and the Sipah Salar, knowing me to be a brother of the Chief of the Kuki Khels, directed me to go and prevail upon Emran to come and make his submission.

"I started out early the next morning for the Safed Koh, and after a long hot climb – for it was nearly midsummer – I found Emran sitting in the shade of a tall pine tree in the midst of his quietly grazing flocks. As I approached he rose and saluted me formally, and enquired whether I and my companions had eaten. When we replied that we had not partaken of any food since setting out at dawn, he disappeared inside his hut and at once put his wife to work preparing a meal for us.

"When Emran had served us with roasted mutton, curds, butter, and white maize bread, which we ate in a little thatched room which served him as a mosque, he turned to me and asked me how it happened that I was passing that way. I explained the whole matter, and urged him to return with me to Kahi Fort to meet the Sipah Salar. Emran answered that he had left his own country in the possession of the Sipah Salar, who could if he wished rule the whole of it from Jalalabad to Nassian. 'For God's sake,' he added, 'let the Sipah Salar rule all that *'ilaqeh* and leave me to tend my flocks in peace. I have no pretensions to a princely title, and I cannot understand why a nobleman such as the Sipah Salar should be anxious to harm me. I am a shepherd, the son of a shepherd, and I hope that my sons will be shepherds when I am gone. It is a worthy calling, and one which I am proud to follow, for as a shepherd I take nothing from any man, but rather provide for the needs of my fellow men – skins, butter, milk and meat. The Sipah Salar, on the other hand, takes everything he finds, even from such a poor house as mine in Nassian.'

"We talked further of the matter, and then I said, 'My Uncle Emran, I understand and appreciate your viewpoint, but, as I have taken service with the Sipah Salar, I must carry out his orders, and if necessary compel you to accompany me to Kahi Fort. But I give you my personal assurance that you will not be harmed, and will be treated with the respect due to a Malik of the Shinwari tribe.

"That night I, together with my five companions, slept in Emran's thatched mosque. Early the following morning Emran approached me, and asked permission to come to Kahi Fort the next day. He took an oath on the Koran that he would present himself at noon before the Sipah Salar. I had to be content with his assurance and went ahead with my followers to report Emran's impending arrival to the Sipah Salar.

"It was arranged that the following day a Durbar, similar to that previously held, should commence at noon in the big courtyard inside Kahi Fort. The Sipah Salar had already taken his seat, and the fourteen Shinwari Maliks had been brought out of captivity to sit once more upon the big crimson carpet in front of the Sipah Salar's chair, when a strange figure was seen approaching through the main gate of the Fort. It was Emran, escorted by two Afghan soldiers, but a different Emran to the one who had been our host on the previous day. This was a shabby ragged figure, in whose beard were sticking pieces of cowdung. I who, before his arrival, had been feeling overjoyed at the thought that it was due to my efforts that Emran had been induced to enter Kahi Fort, was now overcome by shame. What credit will be ascribed to me, I thought, when such a miserable captive makes an appearance in the Sipah Salar's Durbar?

"When Emran's shuffling gait eventually brought him in front of Ghulam Haidar, the latter gazed on him in amazement. 'Are you, Emran?' he asked. Emran replied in little more than a whisper, 'I am, my Lord.'

"The Sipah Salar brooded for a while with his chin on his hand. Eventually he looked up, and said, 'Why did you not appear when I summoned you, Emran?' 'O Lord,' replied Emran, still speaking in the same low tone of voice, 'I thought that these old fools (and here he indicated his fellow-Maliks), and the various other messengers who came to me, were trying to play a practical joke on me. It was beyond my comprehension that a nobleman of your dignity should condescend so low as to wish to make the acquaintance of a humble shepherd. But when my honourable young friend (and here he pointed to me) told me that you really required my presence, I came at once.'

"When the Sipah Salar had heard this explanation, his face, which till then had worn a very severe expression, softened, and speaking in a mild tone of voice he said, 'O Emran, I have indeed wronged you. I see that you are a humble man, interested only in caring for your flocks, and without a wish to harm anyone else. I desire to make reparation for the wrong done to you by my hasty orders. I will therefore undertake to fulfil any desire you may have. Tell me your wish, so that I may order my servants to fulfil it.'

"When Emran heard these words he sighed deeply. 'O Lord,' he said, 'there are many who look to you for the fulfilment of their wishes. Only allow me to retrace my steps to my shepherd's hut and my flocks.' This reply only made the Sipah Salar more anxious to ascertain what wish lay nearest to Emran's heart, and to meet it. The Sipah Salar therefore urged Emran with greater vehemence to declare his wish.

"After a slight pause Emran said, 'Lord, you would not like to fulfil my wish, and I do not desire that posterity should revile your name for having made a promise which you were not willing to carry out.' The Sipah Salar replied, 'You must not ask me for the throne of Afghanistan, for it belongs to my master, the Emir Abdur Rahman Khan. Ask according to your status and position.' Emran then said, 'My Lord, I am a shepherd, but not a fool. My wish will be extremely modest, befitting my status as a Malik of this tribe.'

"The Sipah Salar then said, 'Speak Emran, for I grow weary of your protestations.' Emran then spoke in a clear voice, so that all could hear, 'My Lord, God be praised that the wish that I have cherished for 50 years is at last about to be fulfilled. The only wish I have in the world is publicly to dishonour by an act of gross indecency four out of these fourteen Maliks whom you see before you.'

"A silence like that following a clap of thunder fell on the Sipah Salar and the whole Durbar. I noticed the fourteen Maliks gazing at each other in horrified silence, each one wondering whether he had been chosen as one of the victims of Emran's diabolic wish.

"The Sipah Salar recovered sufficiently to exclaim, 'You rascal, you cannot be in earnest.' Emran, without turning a hair, replied, 'My Lord, do not lose your composure. Even if all these fourteen were to die, it were better than that you should be known to posterity as a breaker of your word.'

"The Sipah Salar took his head in his hands and brooded deeply for a while. Then he looked up and said, 'Well, rascal, since you are set upon this mischief, choose your victims.'

"Emran, in the same composed manner, replied, 'O Lord, if I were to choose in haste I might choose the wrong persons to disgrace. I would rather have a week in which to contemplate my choice. If you permit, we will all meet again at this hour after seven days, by which time I shall have decided which four of this rascally collection – and here he pointed disdainfully to his fellow Maliks – are most deserving of public disgrace.'

"The Sipah Salar saw in this proposal a respite, however brief, from the dire result of the promise he had given. He said therefore, 'I agree, Emran. I will meet you again in full Durbar in one week's time.' Emran requested that till then he and his fellow Maliks might be permitted to return to their homes, leaving their sons as hostages. The Sipah Salar agreed to this request, and the Durbar was brought to an end forthwith.

"Emran went back with a carefree heart to his house in Nassian village. Although his granary was empty and his haystacks gone, he saw no reason to be downcast. In fact one of his neighbours heard him address the scarecrow of a mule, which was the only animal left to welcome him home, as follows, 'Ohé Mushki, soon thy belly shall be sleek and round. Thou shalt be a fit mount for thy worthy master when he rides round his new estates.' When Emran's neighbours were told of his conversation they merely concluded that his disappointment at losing so much of his property, while the Afghan cavalry was in occupation of his village, must have turned his brain.

"The neighbours would have been even more surprised if they had heard the gentle tap which sounded on Emran's door late the following night. It was two of Emran's fellow Maliks. Emran rose up to let them in. He affected to be surprised to see them at that hour of the night. 'How kind of you to come and visit me, my brothers. I presume it is to see the extent of the damage my property suffered while you were living comfortably in Kahi Fort.' The elder of the two Maliks broke in on Emran's words, saying, 'For God's sake, Emran, do not joke with us. We have come to request that, on the appointed day when you choose your victims, you spare us.' Emran replied, 'Some things can be done differently, but this cannot be changed. You are the very two whom I have long had in mind to disgrace. In fact I have decided that it is with you that I shall start.'

"When they heard these words both Maliks fell on the ground and besought Emran, by all that he held dear, to spare them. At length Emran, becoming tired of their supplications, said, 'I will spare you on one condition, which is that you take an oath on the Koran, backed by security of ten thousand rupees, that you will never oppose me, and will never do anything to harm me.' The Maliks were only too thankful to agree to Emran's conditions, and having made their oath and given their security, disappeared into the night as stealthily as they had come.

"The next night, and each night for the rest of the week, two or three of Emran's fellow Maliks paid him a clandestine visit; and by the time the Durbar was due he had obtained a similar oath, backed in each case by security amounting to ten thousand rupees, from each of the Elders of the tribe.

"When the day of the Durbar arrived, all fifteen Maliks assembled in front of the Sipah Salar, who wore an extremely worried look at the thought of the distasteful spectacle which he was going to have to witness. He was, however, determined to get the matter over quickly, so he at once called on Emran to choose his victims.

"Emran rose to his feet and said, 'Lord, when I appeared in the Durbar last week I was so out of humour that I asked you to fulfil a wish which is unsuitable to a man of my age and position. I ask your pardon for that.' On hearing these words the Sipah Salar breathed a sigh of relief, and we noticed that his face shone with pleasure at the thought that Emran had, apparently at the last moment, reconsidered his decision.

"The Sipah Salar, who was anxious to return to Kabul without further delay, saw plainly that the present would be a good opportunity to settle once and for all the affairs of the Shinwari tribe. He therefore addressed the fifteen Maliks and bade them select their Chief. One of the Maliks who (I afterwards learned) had been coached by Emran, said, 'Lord, our chief is Emran.' The Sipah Salar was much surprised at this declaration, and called on the remaining Maliks to say whether they agreed with it. For a while the Maliks remained sitting in silent perplexity, but, when the Sipah Salar insisted that they reply, they assented to the proposal with evident unwillingness and in a subdued tone of voice.

"The Sipah Salar at once gave his official approval to their choice, and declared in full Durbar that Emran was thenceforth to be the Chief of the Sango Khel Shinwaris. He then allocated to Emran, as Chief of the tribe, a *jagir* of four thousand rupees a year, together with the privilege of raising 300 khassadars, who would be paid by the Emir's Government.

"In this manner Emran, after a life of great hardship, rose to opulence and power. 'My child,' my grandfather concluded, 'Emran never troubled to learn even the letters of the alphabet, but, as the poet Sa'di says,

God provides fools in such abundance
that the wise become perplexed.' "

Two

THE STORY OF THE COLONEL'S BITCH

It had been a long march from Mansehra, that winter day, and I reached the little Resthouse under the wall of Oghi Fort long after night had fallen, to learn that the mail lorry had been prevented by the depth of snow on the Pass from reaching Oghi. So I was faced with the prospect of spending the next day or so without even a toothbrush, much less a change of clothes. However, Zarif Khan was there to greet me, and after a supper of *pilau* washed down by green tea, we drew our chairs close to the fire to beguile with conversation the first cold watches of the night.

I have often thought how strange it is that, if Zarif Khan came to England, he would receive a warm welcome at my home, whereas if I ventured into Tirah, where his home lies, I would be shot as dead as mutton by the first Afridi who saw me. This embargo on the entry of Englishmen into Tirah applies even to those who have Afghan blood in their veins. "Such," said Zarif, "was the famous Warburton, whose mother was a Durani princess, and who for many years commanded the Khyber Rifles." "Surely," I said, "there must have been occasions when Colonel Warburton visited the home of one or other of his Afridi officers and men?" "Never, Sahib," Zarif replied, "though it is true that on one occasion an English retriever bitch of his paid a visit to Tirah for several months."

"It happened," Zarif went on, "that a certain Havaldar of the Khyber Rifles, whose name was Gul Mohammad, who had for many years acted as Colonel Warburton's orderly, one day incurred the displeasure of the Colonel, who promptly sent him packing to his home in Tirah. Now the Colonel's favourite retriever bitch was very attached to the orderly, who had taken great pains in training her as a gun-dog, and when she saw Gul Mohammad leaving Landi Kotal Fort she decided to go with him and share his exile. The next day hue and cry for the bitch was raised in the Fort, and an extensive search for her was carried out in the nearby Shinwari villages, but all to no avail. Nor did it occur to anyone that the bitch might have accompanied Gul Mohammad when he left the Fort to return to his home in Tirah.

"A few months later Colonel Warburton took advantage of the fact that a certain Subahdar was going on leave to his home in Gul Mohammad's village, to send a message to him. The message, which was intended to tantalize the ex-Havaldar with memories of plentiful food and (comparatively) easy living in Landi Kotal Fort, was (literally translated from the Pushtu), 'I have forced you to be content to eat yellow maize in the Tirah Hills'.

"To this Gul Mohammad sent back, through the Subahdar, a retort: 'Yellow maize is no novelty to me, for my forefathers were always accustomed to such fare. You should think rather of the fate of your little bitch who, poor animal, leaves my house early each morning in order to lick the millstones where the maize is ground, and returns forlornly every evening with her muzzle covered with white flour, but with her belly still unfilled.'

"Colonel Warburton was both amused at this retort and relieved to know that his retriever was safe. He at once sent a message to Gul Mohammad telling him to return to Landi Kotal. The ex-Havaldar reappeared, as he had departed, with the Colonel's bitch at his heels. Colonel Warburton straightway pardoned Gul Mohammad for his former fault, reinstated him in the Khyber Rifles, and shortly afterwards promoted him to be Jemadar.

"*Sometimes*," added Zarif Khan, quoting the Persian poet Sa'di, "*those of royal blood reward delinquents with a Robe of Honour*."

Three

THE VERSATILITY OF AMIR KHAN AFRIDI

One evening, when Zarif Khan and I had put aside our work, and were refreshing ourselves with green tea in the Resthouse below the wall of Oghi Fort, our conversation turned to the question of versatility, and Zarif remarked, "If you would like to know how versatile an Afridi can be, I will tell you the story of Amir Khan of my own tribe of Kuki Khels, which is famous throughout Tirah."

Zarif was aware what my answer would be, so, after only a brief pause, he went on, "Many years ago the City Magistrate of Peshawar was a Captain Connolly, and his closest friend was the Garrison Engineer, who rejoiced in the name of 'Pukka' Smith, to distinguish him from all the other Smiths in India. Smith had an Afridi orderly, whose name was Amir, who accompanied him on tour everywhere up and down the Frontier. It was Amir who carried the yellow-labelled confidential boxes to and fro between the Garrison Engineer's and the other Government offices, and it was Amir who had for several years been the implicitly-trusted factotum of Smith's office and household.

"Various reports, however, which had found their way into the City Magistrate's files, led Connolly to the conclusion that his friend's orderly was by no means as respectable as his name implied. In fact that extremely well-informed organization, the C.I.D., had made it clear that they suspected Amir of being hand in glove with one of the Afridi gangs which were responsible for the burglaries at that time frequently committed in and around Peshawar Cantonment.

"It was alleged that the fact that Amir was employed in the Garrison Engineer's office enabled him to know exactly when civil and military officers, occupying bungalows in the Cantonment, would be going out on tour or on leave, and that he was passing on this information to his Afridi accomplices, so that they would know which houses would be empty, and therefore safe to burgle. 'Pukka' Smith, however, refused to believe anything which either the magistrate or the police had to say against his orderly.

"One day, when Amir came into the City Magistrate's court-room to deliver a note from his master, Connolly took the opportunity to give Amir a timely warning. Addressing him in Pushtu he said, 'You know as well as I do, Amir, that you are a thorough *badmash*, and though your Sahib refuses to believe the reports made to him, he will one day learn what your real character is; and I warn you, Amir, that if you ever come before me in this Court for the offence of house-breaking, I shall award you the maximum sentence of seven years' rigorous imprisonment.' Amir only smiled broadly and said, 'Let it be seen, Sahib, what happens if I am caught.'

"Later that week a particularly daring burglary was committed on a bungalow on the Mall in Peshawar Cantonment, but this time the police had spread their net wide, and as Amir was entering the wicket-gate into the Garrison Engineer's garden, strong arms caught him in a vice-like grip, and he was hauled summarily to the Police Station. It was found that Amir, with a carelessness astonishing in such an astute criminal, was armed with a revolver, and had, slung over his shoulder, a pair of binoculars, stolen that very night from the bungalow where his accomplices were operating, which he had evidently appropriated on the spot as his share of the loot.

"Amir's guilt could hardly have been clearer, and he was duly produced before the City Magistrate as an accused under the appropriate section of the Indian Penal Code. When Connolly saw Amir his eyes lit up. 'So you have appeared before me earlier than you thought, you rascal,' he said. 'Yes, Sahib,' replied Amir, quite unabashed, 'but it was the Almighty who ordained that the matter should turn out thus, not you.' After which verbal exchange the trial commenced.

"When judgement had been pronounced and Amir had been sentenced to five years' rigorous imprisonment, but before the prisoner had been removed from the courtroom, Connolly addressed Amir as follows: 'Well, rascal, I hope that five years' hard labour will help curb your impudence'; to which Amir replied, 'I am not displeased, Sahib, for to a brave man shackles are as much an ornament as bangles are to a girl; lions and tigers are chained, not jackals.' On hearing these words Connolly flew into a rage, and shouted, 'What, you rascal, are you still insolent after I have passed sentence on you? It seems that the dose I have given you is not sufficient, so I hereby increase it, in fulfilment of my promise, to seven years' rigorous imprisonment.' Amir, was however, quite unperturbed, and answered, 'Be on thy guard, Sahib, lest thou burst! It is not thou that sentencest me but the Law.' Before Amir could make any more sallies of this kind he was bundled out of the courtroom, still chuckling with laughter.

"In those days the North-West Frontier Province was still a part of the Punjab, so Amir had to be sent all the way to Rawalpindi to serve his sentence. It so happened that he and his Police escort reached there in the evening too late for him to be admitted as a convict. He was therefore lodged in the lock-up in the outer enclosure of the jail.

"It was a swelteringly hot July night, and Amir was sweating profusely – so much so that he found that, with a certain amount of persuasion, he was able to slip the manacles over his perspiring wrists. As he did so the manacles made a clinking sound, which led the Sikh warder, who was sitting on a wooden box in the corridor outside, with his back against the bars of the cell door, to call out,

'What are you doing in there, Pathan?' Amir replied at once, 'O Sirdar, I am suffering from a fever, so I shiver.' Then, adopting a wheedling tone, he continued, 'O Sirdar, I know that you are of noble blood. Before the English came you were the masters of the Punjab. You deserve a higher post than looking after convicts in the jail here. You people of noble lineage always take pity on the downfallen. Surely you will have pity on me.' While making this speech Amir was careful to keep his *chadur* well wrapped round him, so that the fact that he had freed his wrists could not be detected.

"A moment or so later another bit of luck came Amir's way. Putting his hand into the pocket of the waistcoat which all Pathans wear, his fingers closed on a lump of opium, which is a drug he sometimes used to soothe his cough. 'Sirdar-ji,' he said, 'would you like to have some opium?' At this the warder snapped, 'Where can opium be found in this hell of a prison?' 'Here is a piece, if you would care to have it,' replied Amir, slipping the lump of opium through the bars. The Sikh took it, crumbled it between his finger nails, and then swallowed it at one gulp. Soon after, a great desire to sleep began to assail him. He sat down again on his box and leaned heavily against the bars of the door. Each time, however, that he nodded off, he at once roused himself from his drowsiness. 'Just like' – as Amir himself told me years later – 'a cock drowsing in the heat of a summer day.' Eventually he fell fast asleep and started to snore. Poor warder! No sooner did Amir hear the first snore than he tentatively tickled the Sikh's ribs, to ascertain whether he had fallen into a really deep slumber. Amir's intention was that, if the warder woke up to find himself being tickled, he would either pretend that he was playing a harmless joke on him, or that he was waking him in case one of the havaldar-warders happened to pass that way. But the opium had produced the desired effect, and Amir's victim was quite unconscious.

"It took only a moment for Amir to put his hand through the bars, unfasten the key from the warder's belt, and unlock the door of the cell. Once outside, he took the manacles by the chain, and swinging them like a flail, he struck the warder a heavy blow on the side of the temple. The latter, uttering a hoarse cry, fell sideways unconscious, and rolled to the ground.

"At the sound of the cry another warder, stationed at the far end of the corridor, called out, 'What is the matter, Ram Singh?' and immediately started running along the passage. Amir realized how desperate his situation was, for in a few moments his escape from the cell would be discovered, and the general alarm raised. He therefore ran as fast as he could along the corridor, which he found led to the main square of the jail. Noticing that a deep rainwater drain ran along one side of the square, he darted into it, and found to his immense relief that, where it tunnelled under the exterior wall of the jail, the iron spikes did not quite reach the floor of the drain. By dint of pressing himself hard against the floor of the channel, and at the cost of a torn shirt and a few scratches, he was able to regain his liberty. As Amir hurried across the fields, he could hear whistles being blown inside the prison, and the big bell being tolled, to warn the jail staff that one of the prisoners had escaped.

"Amir was now faced with the problem of finding his way back to Tirah, on the Afghan side of the Frontier, and he came to the conclusion that, in order to evade recapture, his best plan would be to head south-east rather than north-west, which is the direction in which his home lay.

"Soon after emerging from the prison drain Amir found himself at the edge of a deep ravine, into which he plunged. The rough track at its bottom led towards the south-east, which was the direction in which he had decided he must travel. He therefore followed it, and during the next few days, by walking at night and lying up during the day, he made his way gradually to the town of Jhelum, which lies on either side of the river of that name where it flows away from the hills of Kashmir into the Punjab plain.

"On the outskirts of the town Amir called at the house of a

wealthy Mussulman, and suggested that he should become his guest. When introducing himself Amir produced, for the inspection of his newfound friend, a flawless genealogy, proving a direct line of descent from the Holy Prophet down to himself – Sayyed Amir Shah! The Mussulman, a man of humble origin who had risen to a position of affluence by successfully participating in the Jhelum wood trade, was delighted to have an opportunity to entertain the scion of such a holy family. He therefore gave a feast in honour of Amir and treated him as a favoured guest.

"This pleasant interlude might have been indefinitely prolonged if it had not occurred to Amir that the Punjab Police might well be on the look-out for errant Sayyeds without visible means of support. Amir therefore one day left the wood-merchant's house without saying goodbye to him, and made his way, still going east, towards Sialkot.

"On his arrival there Amir laid out what he had left of the money, given him by the credulous Mussulman, on the purchase of a Hindu Sadhu's yellow robe. He then set about learning a few *mantras* by heart, and how to rotate a brass plate at the tip of a long stick held above his head. The mastery of these simple tricks enabled Amir to pass as a particularly holy Sadhu, and to collect in alms from the Hindu shopkeepers of the Sialkot Bazaar a sum sufficient to pay for his onward journey to Kashmir.

"The next stage of Amir's journey took him to Baramula, a small town of wooden houses interspersed with poplar trees, which stands at the edge of the mountain-encircled Wular Lake, at the western end of the Vale of Kashmir.

"Amir had found it far more lucrative to pose as a Sadhu than as a Sayyed, so on his arrival in Baramula he lost no time in clothing himself once more in his yellow robe. He found life in Baramula much to his liking, because during the day the various Brahman Pundits, with whom he found lodging, fed him and gave him alms, and during the night the Pundits' comely daughters lavished their caresses on him. I do not wonder at this," said Zarif, "because

Amir was a remarkably handsome man, with a fine bold look, and the classical features which crop up from time to time in north-western India, seemingly as a legacy from the invasion of Alexander the Great.

"There is, however, a Pushtu saying that 'To every man his own country is Kashmir', and after a while Amir started to feel homesick for the bare and inhospitable hills of Tirah. Early one morning, therefore, he set out once more upon his travels. He took the road which winds down, through a tangle of wild mountain valleys in a south-westerly direction towards Garhi Habibullah. This time he adopted the dress of a well-to-do Kabuli *émigré* – one of the many Afghan noblemen who went into exile when Emir Abdur Rahman ascended the throne of Afghanistan.

"On arrival at the little riverside town of Garhi, Amir tried out on its stout and affable Khan the ruse to which these gentry were much addicted. Having gained the Khan's confidence, he led him to understand that he had a beautiful wife and a daughter 'slim as a moon of Ramadan', whom he wished to leave under his protection while he was away visiting friends at Ludhiana, on the far side of the Punjab. The Khan, who was of a sensitive disposition, had no sooner heard the details of the proposed arrangement than his moustache started to quiver and his ears to twitch. Amir, noticing these promising signs, decided that the time was ripe to ask for the loan of a hundred rupees. This sum the Khan gladly entrusted to him, and Amir went on his way rejoicing.

"Amir decided that he might run some danger of being recaptured if he travelled directly by the highway through Mansehra and Abbottabad. Instead he struck across country to Darband, and made his way to the ferry at Pehure, where he planned to cross the Indus undetected into Swabi Tehsil. It happened, however, that while waiting for the ferry, he overheard some boatmen discussing the reward which had been offered by the police for his apprehension. He detected in their conversation what seemed to him a morbid anxiety to be in a position to claim the reward, so he decided that it would be worth making a wide detour in order to cross the river in safety.

"Amir therefore retraced his steps northward, and passing once more through Darband, made his way to the ferry at Thakot in Hazara Tribal Territory, which is where Alexander the Great crossed the Indus with his army. He got safely over the ferry into Swat, and from there passed through Tribal Territory to the Khyber Pass. Arrived there, he lost no time in slipping across the border into Afghanistan, and soon after arrived back at his home in Tirah.

"On his arrival in his own village Amir was disappointed to find that, so far from being fêted as a returned hero after his resourceful escape from prison and his subsequent adventures, he was cold-shouldered by his relatives, one of whom said to him, 'Where, O Son of a Henpecked Father, have you been hiding during the past twelve months?'

"It did not take Amir long to realize that it had been a great mistake to exchange the comfortable life he had enjoyed in Kashmir for his present existence among his fellow-countrymen, whose manners were uncouth, and whose daily fare, consisting of roughly-ground maize bread, was unsuited to his now more sophisticated taste. He therefore began to cast about in his mind for some means by which to provide himself with a more palatable diet. And this is what led Amir to embark on a career of highway robbery. Not that that is how he would at first have described his new vocation. He merely walked a couple of miles along a track leading from his own village of Sirkai, and having chosen a suitable site, collected a quantity of large stones, which he used to construct a small *sangar*. Upon the protective wall nearest to the track leading to Sirkai be mounted an ancient blunderbuss, with a barrel some nine feet long, which was capable of firing a ball of lead about the size of a walnut. To enable this weapon to achieve a sufficiently deadly muzzle velocity he had to wrap its bullet in a piece of cloth. Amir found, too, that when the gun was fired, the barrel was liable to part company from the stock, so, taking advantage of the sacrifice of a bullock at the *'Id*, he obtained from the animal's owner the loan of its tendons, which he used to bind the barrel of the gun firmly to its wooden stock. To this ferocious-looking piece of artillery Amir gave the name *Jahan Panah*, which means 'Terror of the World'.

"It is necessary to explain," Mohammed Zarif went on, "that Amir, so far from intending to terrify the whole world, in fact preyed only on such persons as he felt sure would willingly pay tribute to *Jahan Panah*. His victims were, therefore, either very old or were suffering from some physical infirmity. Nevertheless their contributions sufficed to enable him at the end of each day, after he had dismantled *Jahan Panah* and laboriously carried it home, to have for supper a whole chicken cooked in butter.

"The delicious smell of a chicken being cooked, which was wafted every evening from Amir's hut, excited the interest of an old crone, who lived nearby. One day she approached him and said, 'My Son Amir, how do you manage to provide yourself with the luxury of a chicken each night?' Amir answered, 'Mother, you should not try to probe the affairs of those whom Fate has afflicted. As you know, through a mischance I lost my job with a Sahib down in Peshawar, and only with great difficulty managed to escape from jail. Now, being unable to accustom myself to the food you people eat, I have been driven to highway robbery.'

"The old woman, far from being dismayed at this disclosure, begged Amir to take her son into partnership with him. 'He is a strong young man,' she assured him, 'and will stand you in good stead. Then,' she added, 'he and I will eat a chicken cooked in butter every evening, just as you do.'

"Amir tried to reason with her, and to persuade her that his was not the sort of calling a young man should elect to follow. 'Your son,' he told her, 'would do far better to go down to Peshawar, and present himself to the Recruiting Officer for enlistment in the Indian Army.' But the old woman was deaf to reason, and continued to demand that her son should be accepted by Amir for training as a highway robber.

"The following morning Amir, having hoisted *Jahan Panah* on to his shoulders, set out for the *sangar*. As he was leaving the outskirts of the village, he happened to look back and saw the old woman and her son hurrying along behind him. When she drew close she started to abuse Amir for refusing to take her son with him. Amir was understandably reluctant to have to share his 'earnings' with anyone else, but the old woman's persistence was such that he eventually agreed to accept her son as his assistant, relieved to think that he would at least be able to shift the weight of *Jahan Panah* on to the lad's willing shoulders. Thus it was that, not long after, Amir reached the *sangar* accompanied by the young man.

"It was a beautiful spring day, and the sun was by now high in the heavens. What a pleasant change it would be, thought Amir, if instead of actively earning my living, I were to drowse for an hour or so in the sunshine inside the *sangar*. He accordingly mounted *Jahan Panah* on the wall of the *sangar*, and having carefully instructed his young assistant that, if anyone were to come into view, he must wake him by very gently pulling his big toe, Amir lay down, drew his *chadur* across his face, and composed himself to sleep.

"It was not long before the boy noticed in the distance a man coming along the path towards the *sangar*. In accordance with his instructions he pulled Amir's big toe, and Amir opened his eyes, threw off the *chadur*, and sat up. The boy, wild-eyed with excitement, told Amir that he had sighted a prospective victim. Amir, well aware of the need for caution, got to his feet, and looked carefully through a chink in the *sangar* wall. He saw clearly that the approaching stranger was an Afridi of ferocious mien from the high plateau of Tirah. He therefore told the boy not to challenge him, and lay down once more in the sun, with the *chadur* over his face.

"It so happened that, at the very moment when the stranger was about to pass the *sangar*, the boy, who was of a very excitable disposition, called out to him to stand and deliver whatever money he had with him. The passerby would probably have ignored the challenge of a mere stripling, but the sound of the boy's voice challenging the stranger had the effect of glavanizing Amir to life. He sprang to the wall of the *sangar* and swung *Jahan Panah* so that it pointed straight at the Afridi. 'You Son of a Devil,' he shouted, 'don't you understand when you are told to deliver your money? Unless you obey you are as good as dead.' The stranger merely stared back insolently, and replied that, as he had neither dishonoured Amir's wife, nor killed his father, there could be no possible reason for Amir to fire at him. While he was speaking the Afridi continued to advance closer to the *sangar*. When it was almost too late, Amir realized the danger that threatened him, and made a clumsy attempt to fire the cap. Before he could do so the Afridi was on him and had caught hold of the barrel with both his hands. Amir, too, seized hold of it, and as they started to struggle he shouted at the stranger. 'You Son of a Devil, you are trying to destroy my *Jahan Panah*. If you take yourself off at once I promise not to harm you.'

"The stranger had, however, no intention of releasing his hold on *Jahan Panah*, and, as he and Amir continued to struggle for its possession, the gun started to emit plaintive squeaks as the tendons that held it together stretched and gave way. Matters were becoming so desperate that Amir called out to his young helper to pick a stone off the wall of the *sangar* and throw it at his adversary. The boy caught hold of a fair-sized boulder, and aiming at the stranger's head, hurled it at him with all his strength. The stranger, however, noticed the boy taking aim, and ducked, with the result that the boulder struck Amir's shoulder with a heavy thud, hurting him so much that he let go of *Jahan Panah*'s barrel with a cry of pain.

"Amir told me long afterwards that the stranger then acted like a military automaton, in stepping three paces smartly backward, and aiming the gun straight at him. Amir, seeing death staring him in the face, involuntarily seized hold of the boy, and swung him in front of him at the very moment when *Jahan Panah* with a loud explosion discharged its bullet. Alas, it found a lodging in the chest of the young man, who fell dead without uttering so much as a moan.

"Without further ado the stranger lifted *Jahan Panah* on to his shoulders, and started off down the track. As soon as Amir realized that the Afridi was making off with his artillery he called out to him, 'O Fool, the lad you have just killed is one of a large family who will exact from you the price of his life in blood. If you carry away this gun you will certainly be traced, but if you leave it here I shall say that I have never set eyes on you. I will think of you only as a brave son of a brave father. Let Afridi mothers always bring forth sons like you!' On hearing these words, the stranger stopped and pondered for a moment or so. Then, putting *Jahan Panah* down on a large rock beside the path, he continued on his way.

"Amir had in his pockets a supply of ammunition sufficient for a whole day's highway robbery, so as soon as he saw that the Afridi had decided to continue his journey without *Jahan Panah*, he scrambled out of the *sangar* and hurried towards the gun, hoping to have time to reload and fire it before the Afridi got out of range, and by killing him to avenge the death of the poor widow's son.

"Before Amir could carry his plan into effect the Afridi who, it seems, had had second thoughts about abandoning *Jahan Panah*, had caught hold of the muzzle of the gun, and had started to batter it with all his might against the large rock upon which he had set it down.

"When Amir saw what was happening he shouted out, 'O Son of a Devil, what are you doing to my gun now?' The stranger, pausing briefly in his work of destruction, gave Amir a pitying smile, and said, 'You cannot fool me. Go and try your tricks elsewhere.' Then, raising *Jahan Panah* high in the air, he brought it down on the rock with a resounding crash. The tendons holding the gun together burst asunder, and the stock, no longer attached to the barrel, flew off and landed among the rocks far away in the valley below. The stranger tossed the barrel after the stock and, without another word, left Amir, this time for good.

"When Amir brought the boy's body back to Sirkai, his mother, in great sorrow and anger, accused him of having caused the death of her son. 'You should not blame me,' replied Amir, 'but the chickens, cooked in butter, which you hoped to enjoy as a result of our partnership.'

"About a year later Amir, in spite of having experienced the hazards of a career of highway robbery, had found no other equally congenial way of earning his living among the bare hills of Tirah. It was at about this time that a Jirga of Afridi Elders requested the Chief Commissioner, Peshawar, to permit Amir to re-enter British India. Their request was granted and Amir soon after arrived back in Peshawar – though what Captain Connolly said to him in Pushtu when he reached there, and with what bold witticisms Amir contrived to answer him, history, alas, does not relate."

Four

THE TALE OF THE EMIR'S SWORD

"During the latter part of the nineteenth century," began Zarif Khan one evening, stirring his green tea with a silver spoon, "at the time when the rivalry between the Emir Sher 'Ali Khan and Mohammad Afzal Khan was at its height, the Emir of Afghanistan sent a summons to the jirga of the Kuki Khel Afridis. The tribesmen reached the capital after a journey of seven days from their homes in Tirah, and on the following day attended the Emir's Durbar in the *Arg* at Kabul.

"For their ceremonial meeting with the Emir, the members of the jirga wore their best clothes, consisting of an embroidered green waistcoat over a clean white shirt, with baggy white pyjamas; and because it was winter each carried wrapped round his shoulders a voluminous blanket to protect him from the cold. When the tribesmen had seated themselves on the big carpet in the inner courtyard of the Citadel, the Emir made his entry with suitable pomp, and the whole Durbar rose and made a deep obeisance to him. He sat down immediately in front of the jirga and bade them all be seated.

"The Emir was anxious to win the Afridis to his side, so he addressed them in a very friendly fashion, ending with the words, 'If I were to have but one half loaf of bread, I would share it with you, my brothers.' When he had finished speaking one of the Elders, named Sher Afzal, rose to his feet and said, '*'Ala Hazrat*, we have seen in Kabul much of the glory of your Kingdom; why then do you speak to us of half loaves? We know that you are the master of many treasuries, and are the king of a great country. If it ever happens, which God forbid, that you possess only half a loaf, we poor tribesmen out of our scanty provisions will give you bread to eat. The present time, while you are king and we are poor, is the proper moment for you to bestow rich gifts upon us.'

"The Emir was very angry that his kind words had been treated so lightly, and he retorted, 'You Son of Satan, I am beset on either side by the rulers of two powerful kingdoms, who have their eyes fixed on this small stretch of land. I am gathering strength for the hour when one of them attacks me. On that day come to me, and I will be liberal in my generosity to you.' Sher Afzal answered, '*'Ala Hazrat*, at this time when your kingdom is at peace and there is ample time for eating, you give us nothing, while you and your Kabuli Wazirs live in the greatest luxury. On the day that your kingdom is soaked in blood you will have to excuse us, for then there will be no time for eating.'

"The Emir was so infuriated by this reply that he rose in haste, and strode unceremoniously out of the Durbar, leaving behind on the carpet beside his chair his sabre in its gold-encrusted scabbard. Now the Afridi who had been seated nearest to the Emir's chair was a certain Amin Khan who, when he noticed that the Emir had left his sword behind, stealthily slipped it beneath the folds of his blanket. Then having made sure that his action had not been noticed, he rose and joined his fellow-tribesmen as they left the courtyard.

"Amin Khan's position at the very edge of the carpet, and the unhurried manner in which he had secured the sword, caused him to be the last member of the jirga to file through the gate of the *Arg*. Unfortunately for Amin a vigilant sentry was on duty there. This man noticed a gleam of gold where the point of the curved scabbard protruded from the folds of the blanket. He therefore seized the Afridi by the arm, tore the blanket from his shoulder, and exposed the sword to view. Amin struggled desperately to free himself, but to no avail. At the sentry's urgent cry for help the Commander of the Guard came running with the other soldiers, and Amin was quickly overpowered.

"The Guard Commander, confident that his sovereign would reward him generously for recovering his sword and arresting the man who had had the effrontery to steal it, took Amin at once into the presence of the king. When the Emir had heard exactly how his sword had been stolen, he flew into a terrible rage, and shouted at Amin, 'You Afridis are just as wicked in your ways as you are in your talk. You Son of Satan, there is no crime worse than to bite the hand that has fed you. I therefore order you to be blown from a gun this evening as soon as the sun has set. There, in the place of execution, the pariah dogs shall feast upon the shreds of your flesh.' Amin Khan, seeing that no appeal for mercy would alter the Emir's decision to destroy him, remained silent, and at a nod from the Emir he was led away.

"Amin was taken from the *Arg* straight to the mound just outside the city wall where, in those days, stood a piece of artillery much used by the Emir for the execution of criminals. Amin's wrists were securely tied to posts on either side of the gun, and he was left with the muzzle of the gun poked hard against his stomach. An hour or so remained till sunset, and Amin looked forward to spending them in acute discomfort.

"A little before sunset, when the shadows were already lengthening across the hills, a member of the jirga named Agha Jan, with whom Amin Khan had long been at enmity, happened to take a stroll outside the wall of the city. When he came to the mound he was astonished to see Amin tied to the gun of execution, and called out to him, 'Amin Khan, what are you doing?' Amin turned his head towards his fellow-tribesman and replied in a calm tone of voice, 'I am committing an impropriety with this unspeakable gun, which has blasted the lives of many Afghans. I am busy. Go your way. I will follow you soon.' Agha Jan was deeply perplexed by these strange words, and drawing closer, said, 'What has happened to you? Surely you are not doing this for pleasure?' Amin Khan replied, 'For God's sake leave me alone. This is no time to disturb me.'

"Agha Jan now realized the gravity of the situation, and he set off at once for the Caravanserai where the Afridi jirga was staying. There he reported to the Khan how he had found Amin fastened to the gun of execution, and the strange words uttered by him. When the members of the jirga realized the terrible fate which was about to overtake Amin a deep despondency fell on them all. The Khan, however, at once rose to his feet and hurried to the *Arg* to seek an audience with the Emir, for he knew that the order for Amin's execution could have been given only by the king himself.

"The Khan, on reaching the *Arg*, made his obesiance to the Emir, and cried out, 'O *'Ala Hazrat*, it is not customary for a member of the jirga to be blown from a gun.' The Emir replied, 'I am executing the man for stealing my sword.' The Khan answered, 'O King, you know well that we Afridis can resist every sort of temptation save that of securing a worthy weapon, and the possibility of acquiring thy sword, O King, would tempt even me from the path of righteousness.' The Khan's words greatly pleased the Emir, and, after pondering for a few moments, he called one of his *ghulambachehs* to his side and ordered him to go straight to the Commander of the Executioners, and tell him to release the Afridi who was due to be blown from the gun at sunset.

"The Khan returned, well pleased, to the Caravanserai, where he told the members of the jirga the happy news of Amin's impending release. When Amin reached the Serai, the Khan spoke to him severely. 'O Amin,' he said, 'how foolish you were not to send word to one of our tribe that your life was in danger. And when Agha Jan chanced to pass by, and asked you what had happened, why did you give him such a rough and meaningless answer?' Amin replied, 'Khan, have you forgotten the old Pushtu verse which runs,

Let me be buried in an unknown grave,
But never let men think I was not brave . . . ?

I did not wish Agha Jan, whose family has a longstanding feud with mine, to be able to boast that he had saved my life. I preferred, O my Father, death to such a fate as that.' "

Five

THE OTHER CHEEK

"One summer day," said Zarif Khan, "I was sitting on a charpoy in the shade of a big walnut tree beside the track that runs from my own country towards Maidan – a village famous for its weekly market, to which Afridis come from all over Tirah – when one of my fellow-tribesmen, whose name was Alamat, passed by leading a mule loaded with torchwood. I could see that he was a very old man, and too weak to be able easily to undertake a long and arduous journey; so when he paused to speak to me I asked him to tell me where he was going, and to whom he intended to deliver his load of wood.

"The ancient answered, 'O Khan, when I was a young man I suffered an ignominious defeat at the hands of a man belonging to a rival tribe, the Malakdin Khel.' When I asked him how this had happened he answered, 'One evening long ago, at a time when the *'Id* was approaching, I came home to be greeted by my wife with curses for not having brought with me any stuff for her to make into new clothes for herself and our children to wear at the Festival. According to the proverb, 'Man is ruled by Woman', so I went the next morning to a nearby shop, owned by a Hindu, and asked him to let me have some cloth on credit, but he refused my request.

"'I returned that evening much cast down in mind by the meagreness of my resources and the fear that my wife would again curse me for being a good-for-nothing husband. When, therefore,

I entered the house, and before my wife could utter a word, I said, "Dear wife, you must not be cross that I have again returned empty-handed. Tomorrow, if God wills, I shall bring home a big bundle of cloth." My wife answered, "All right, you miserable fellow, let us see what you will bring. I can make do with my old clothes, but our little son and daughter must certainly have new clothes for the *'Id*."

"'On leaving our house early the next morning, I walked as far as the main track that runs beside the Bara River, and having collected from the river-bed some large round stones for use as ammunition. I sat down in the shade of a tree to wait for someone carrying a bundle of cloth to come by.

"'I did not have long to wait before I saw in the distance a man with a donkey coming along the track from the direction of Peshawar. In order not to alarm my prospective victim I lay down under the tree and covered my face with my *chadur*, but when the sound of footsteps told me that the man was close at hand, I sprang to my feet and, without a moment's hesitation, hurled one of the stones at him. It struck him in the ribs, and caused the poor fellow to groan aloud. Before he could utter a word I shouted at him, "Don't move, you rascal, there's another stone coming." He answered, moaning with pain, "For God's sake tell me why you are behaving so cruelly when I have never wronged you in any way."

"'I shouted back at him, "Don't you understand, you rascal, that I intend to rob you of the bundle of cloth you are carrying on your donkey?" He answered, "If it is cloth you need take the whole load, but do not throw any more stones at me." I had no intention of forbearing because of his entreaties, and I at once hurled another stone at him, which struck him in the small of his back. The unfortunate man reeled under the impact of this further blow and cried out to me, "You brute, you are the son not of a man but a devil. Why, when I make no resistance, do you continue to pelt me with stones?" I replied, "Robbery must be accompanied by violence; if it isn't, my action in taking your cloth will look like that of a beggar receiving alms." When the stranger saw that I was not going to relent because of his entreaties he made off towards his home. As soon as he was out of sight I removed the load of cloth from his donkey and left the animal there.

"'I returned home with a light heart, and on entering my house threw down the bale of stuff in front of my wife, crying out as I did so, "Here is the cloth you asked for: make as many garments for yourself and your relatives as you want: admit that I am an expert thrower-of-stones, and never again call me an unworthy husband!" I then related the whole story of how the cloth had come into my possession, and my wife raised no objection to the way in which I had acquired it.

"'Towards the end of that summer my wife asked me to take our donkey to fetch a load of red beans from the market at Maidan, and I set out with a few rupees in my pocket early the next morning. I had spent some time wandering from booth to booth in the shade of the *chenar* trees, trying to decide which were the best beans to buy, when a heavy hand fell on my shoulder. I looked round, and saw to my horror the very man whom I had robbed a few months earlier.

"'At first I was so dumbfounded that I was unable to answer his salutation, but on regaining my composure I held out my hand to shake his. He said to me, "Brother, what are you purchasing?" I replied, "Beans." "This year," he said, "I have harvested a lot of beans. You must not buy any here. I will give you as many as you need." "No," I said, "please allow me to purchase them in the market." He then said, "I trust that you will not gainsay my wishes. Where is your donkey standing? You will be accompanying me with your donkey to my house, which is nearby." 'I saw,' said Alamat, 'that I had no alternative but to go with him, for the market was full of his fellow-tribesmen, who would undoubtedly have torn me to pieces if he had given the word.

"'So it was that I and my donkey left the market in the company of the stranger, and after walking a mile with him, reached his house. There he called to his mother to bring out a charpoy and cover it with a blanket for me to sit on. He told his mother to prepare a meal, and it was not long before an elaborate supper was laid before me. That night they gave me good clean bedding to sleep on, and the next morning provided a breakfast of hot milk and maize bread. In fact they overwhelmed me with every sort of hospitality, and all the while I kept wondering why this stranger should be showing such kindness to me.

"'As soon as breakfast was over, in order to put an end to my suspense I said, "Please put the beans in my saddlebags, so that I may depart." My host replied, "Stay two more days with us; today I am going to bring back a load or ripe peaches from the orchard of my maternal uncle, and we will enjoy eating them together." I cut short his kind words by saying, "I beseech you to load my donkey and tell me what price you will accept for the beans." At that he told his mother to fill my donkey's saddlebags, but when I again offered to pay for the load he said, "I am not a Hindu, and I have not opened a shop in order to dispose of my beans for money. I have treated you as a brother, and I am giving the beans to you as a present."

"'With these words echoing in my ears I set off with my donkey on my homeward journey. My host accompanied me to the edge of his fields, and there he shook hands with me and bade me farewell. After he had done so I walked a few steps, and then stopped, and turned round and said to him, "Have you recognized who I am?" He answered curtly, "Yes." 'Then,' said Alamat, 'I became as if spellbound, and my lips seemed too numbed to be able to utter a word. At last I managed to say, "Do you think that I can possibly accept your beans when I have so ill-treated you?" The man replied, "You MUST accept these beans. I have a rifle in my hand and thirty cartridges in my bandolier. I do not care who you are, but if you leave the beans here I will certainly shoot you. I have been instructing you how a man ought to behave towards his fellow men. You certainly need teaching."

"Alamat, seeing no other course open to him, without another word led away his donkey with its load of beans. 'Since then,' said Alamat, 'I have never practised any kind of robbery. Indeed, every year I have fetched two loads of torchwood from the pine forest far up on the slopes of the Safed Koh and delivered them at the house of my mentor. I am, as you see, an old man now, and I would willingly be rid of this obligation. But alas, my son who has grown up to be a strong young man only laughs at me, instead of relieving me of the burden of this task. And yet,' Alamat added, 'it was in order to clothe him and his sister that I committed the crime which I have been expiating ever since.'

"Our Pushtu proverb," said Zarif Khan, smiling broadly, "is certainly true which says,

There is no need to give poison to someone whom sweetness will destroy."

Six

THE UNPROFITABLE PRISONER

And those who harvested the Golden Grain
And those who flung it to the Winds like Rain. . . .
Edward FitzGerald's *Rubáiyát of Omar Khayyám*

One evening at Oghi, when Zarif Khan and I had finished discussing the complex problems of the Hazara Tribal Area, and the relevant files had been packed away in the *yakdan* in which they had travelled with me from Mansehra, it happened that Zarif's thoughts turned to his own people, the Afridis who inhabit the mountainous area of Tirah between Peshawar and the frontier of Afghanistan.

"As you know," said Zarif, "the Afridis are divided into eight Clans, every one of which has its own Chief. During the nineteenth century each Clan maintained a feud with its nearest neighbour, the leaders in this rivalry being the Kuki Khels, to which I belong, and the Malakdin Khels. In order to intensify the feud, the young men of each Clan used to play a game of capturing or killing those of the rival Clan. Geographically the advantage lay with us, because the Kuki Khel area between High Tirah and Peshawar lies close to the Khyber Pass, so a Malakdin Khel tribesman travelling to Peshawar could not avoid passing through our territory.

"There is only one track through the mountains, and it follows the windings of the Bara River. Nearly every one of the river's twists and turns provides a blind corner, suitable for an ambush. At such corners the young men of the Kuki Khel used to amuse themselves by lying in wait for unwary passers-by. One of them, a man of insignificant appearance named Gul Hassan, was particularly addicted to this form of sport. He had chosen as collaborator a stalwart young man named Rahim, and together they used to sit up at night beside the track, in the hope of being lucky enough to surprise and capture some member of the Malakdin Khel tribe.

"This pastime was brought to an abrupt conclusion early one morning when, after a night spent fruitlessly in ambush, Rahim had gone off in search of water for his ablutions preparatory to saying his morning prayers, leaving his friend standing alone beside the track.

"It was at this moment that Gul Hassan saw a tall and ferocious-looking man striding along the path towards him. Realizing the danger of confronting such a person, Gul Hassan crouched down behind a big boulder, hoping that the stranger would pass by without noticing him. When, however, the man drew nearer, and was about to pass the spot where Gul Hassan lay concealed, Gul Hassan began to think it would be a pity if such a fine specimen were allowed to pass unchallenged, especially as Rahim might at any moment arrive back in time to help him. Gul Hassan therefore suddenly sprang on to the boulder behind which he had been hiding, and shouted out, 'Stop, and tell me to which Khel you belong – otherwise you are a dead man!' At the same time Gul Hassan placed his hand threateningly on the butt of his pistol.

"When the stranger heard these words and noticed the diminutive Gul Hassan standing on the boulder, he called out, 'What do you want, my boy?' Gul Hassan then took a deep breath, and shouted back as loudly as he could (for he hoped that Rahim might be able to hear him), 'If you hesitate to surrender to me I shall send you instantly to be a guest of the Dead of your Clan.'

"The tall stranger laughed softly, and then answered in a

composed manner, 'You seem to be a very naughty boy. Do you want me to give you a lift to my home?' Saying which, he moved towards Gul Hassan who, astonished by such nonchalance, did not stir till he felt the grip of the stranger's fingers on his arm.

"Gul Hassan (still hoping to make Rahim hear) shouted in an even louder voice, 'How dare you lay hands on me while I am standing on ground owned by my Clan?' The stranger replied, 'It is your fault, not mine. It is you who challenged me. I am therefore going to take you to my house, where I shall keep you a prisoner until your family sends me a large sum of money to pay for your release.'

"Without further ado the gigantic stranger jerked Gul Hassan off his feet, flung him over his shoulder, and strode off in the direction of his home. After Gul Hassan had been carried like this for a few paces he recovered his wits, and called on his captor to tell him where he was taking him. The stranger replied, 'Keep your tongue from talking, and your hands and feet from moving, or I will throw you over a precipice into the Bara River.'

"Gul Hassan accordingly remained silent and motionless till the cliffs of the Bara gorge were behind them and the track had started to run through level country, raised two or three feet above the ploughed fields on either hand. By dint of wriggling on to one side, Gul Hassan managed to draw his pistol from his belt and cock it. He then pressed the muzzle of the pistol against the back of the stranger's head, and called out to him, 'Throw me down, you rascal, or I will shatter your skull.' The stranger, feeling the muzzle of the pistol against his neck, stopped suddenly, flexed his shoulders, and then, with a tremendous jerk, flung Gul Hassan down into the ploughed field.

"Gul Hassan fell headlong, and the pistol, escaping from his grasp, buried itself in the earth without going off. Gul Hassan quickly recovered his weapon, and running parallel with the stranger, started shouting to some nearby huts, which he knew to be inhabited by his fellow clansmen. 'Come and help me,' he cried, 'for alone I cannot overpower this devil.' Two or three villagers, who had been praying in the mosque, came running out with their rifles, and quickly made the giant a prisoner.

"The villagers tied the stranger's hands securely behind his back, and bade him return along the track with Gul Hassan. When they reached the spot where Gul Hassan had first challenged the stranger they found Rahim sitting on top of the big boulder. When he saw Gul Hassan approaching with his prisoner in tow he called out to congratulate him on the capture of such a fine specimen of the rival Clan. Gul Hassan replied, 'May your father burn forever! Where were you when I was caught by this giant?' Rahim replied gently, 'Forgive me, brother, I was out of earshot down in the ravine. In any case, you alone have had the glory of capturing him. Let us now go home.'

"They took the stranger, still bound, to Gul Hassan's house, where, after giving him some maize-bread and some milk, they left him tied up in the cowbyre below the living-room of the house. Gul Hassan then climbed up to the living-room, where he regaled his wife with the astonishing story of how he had overpowered the giant and brought him home as his captive. When, however, Gul Hassan and his wife retired to bed they were startled to hear a series of shrieks and groans from the room below, accompanied by loud thumps on the joists supporting the ceiling. After they had been woken up serveral times in this manner Gul Hassan called out, 'Hi, you rascal down there, are you not going to allow us to have any sleep tonight?' The stranger answered, 'What kindness have you done me that I should allow you to sleep? You have left me here with your cows and their fleas as my companions, so why should I allow you to sleep in peace?'

"The remainder of the night passed in a similar fashion, and when morning came Gul Hassan again remonstrated with his captive for disturbing his night's rest. The stranger replied, 'You should treat me as a man, and not as an animal. From now on you are going to learn what trouble you have called down on your head for making me spend the night with your cows.'

"Gul Hassan considered these remarks, and decided that, for the sake of peace at night, he would in future confine his prisoner in the third storey of the house, which in Tirah is the one ordinarily used for the storage of grain and dried vegetables. In this room Gul Hassan placed a charpoy, a mattress, and a blanket, together with a pitcher of water for the stranger's use, and here Gul Hassan locked his prisoner each night.

"After a week had passed, during which the stranger had enjoyed a daily diet of maize-bread, boiled vegetables, and curds, Gul Hassan broached the subject of his ransom. He told the stranger that a Hindu shopkeeper in the village would shortly be leaving for the country of the Malakdin Khel, and that he could carry a message from the stranger to his relatives. The stranger replied that he had no relatives or friends in his own country who would be willing to pay any money as ransom for him, and that there was therefore no point in sending a message by the Hindu. He added that he was willing to stay with Gul Hassan as long as he, Gul Hassan, wished to keep him.

"After a further week had passed, Gul Hassan suggested to his captive that his health would suffer if he were to continue sitting idly in the upper room of the house. He suggested that the stranger might go for a walk of a mile or so every day in any direction he liked. Gul Hassan hoped, by providing such opportunities to escape, to be rid of his guest, whose hearty appetite was proving a strain on his slender resources.

"The stranger took Gul Hassan's advice, and every day went out for a long walk, which if anything increased his appetite. He returned regularaly at sunset each day with a small bundle of faggots tied in the end of his turban, which he had collected to burn in the fireplace in the upper room.

"Since in Tirah custom and personal honour alike forbid the killing or dishonouring of a captive, Gul Hassan was more than ever perplexed by the problem of what to do with his prisoner. He next suggested that the stranger might perhaps be finding it inconvenient to return every evening to his house. Gul Hassan therefore proposed to him that he might care sometimes to spend a night or so away, enjoying the hospitality of some of the other Kuki Khel families. The stranger thanked him for the kind thought but said that, as he was Gul Hassan's captive, it was incumbent on him to return every evening to his house. 'After all,' he said, 'you have put your trust in me, and I cannot betray it.'

"Gul Hassan saw that the time had come to speak plainly, so he told the stranger the story of the man who jumped into the river to try to catch hold of a black blanket, which appeared to be floating by but which was in fact a black bear swimming in the river. People on the bank shouted to the man to leave the blanket if he could not pull it out, and he called back that he was ready to leave the blanket, but that the blanket would not let go of him. 'You,' he told the stranger, 'are that same blanket that will not let me go. For the sake of our fathers' souls, I beg you to leave my house and return to your own country.' The stranger replied, 'Gul Hassan, I cannot understand how you can wish to violate the sacred rules of Afridi hospitality by trying to make me quit your house. Surely you realize that it is my privilege to leave your house when I wish.'

"Not long after this Gul Hassan's wife, returning early one morning with a pitcher of water from the well, noticed that all the chickens of the village were clustered in front of the house, and were busily pecking at the grain strewn there. Looking up, she noticed that a rope was hanging from a beam that jutted from the top storey of the house. She hurried inside, and climbed the ladder to their captive's room. She found the door still chained outside, and the room itself as bare as a mosque. The stranger had evidently escaped by plaiting a rope of rushes pulled out of the charpoy.

"Before departing, the stranger had flung broadcast the whole of Gul Hassan's supply of maize, wheat, and dried vegetables, which had been stored in the upper chamber as provision against the coming winter. Moreover he had hurled all the earthenware pitchers far down into the stream that flowed below the village.

"When Gul Hassan, summoned from his bed to the upper room by his wife's cries, saw the extent of the damage, he was amazed. He calculated that the stranger must have spent at least two hours industriously carrying basket-loads of grain up to the roof of the house, in order to scatter it in such a way that it could never be recovered. Gul Hassan laughed bitterly when he saw how efficiently his captive had disposed of his granary. 'Wife,' he said, 'that is the last man I ever catch alive.'

"A few years later Gul Hassan met the stranger once more. They were both staying at the Mullah Serai which is close to the Bajauri Gate of Peshawar City. Recognition was mutual, and after they had formally saluted each other, Gul Hassan complained of the unmannerly fashion of the other's departure from his house. The stranger replied, 'O Gul Hassan, you ought not to be downcast, for now we are equal. You lost your grain, but I – I had to spend a night with your cows. Remember, my friend, our Pushtu proverb,

Who has no grain will never know the pest
That others suffer – the unwanted guest.'"

Seven

THE DEATH OF AN OUTLAW

The dead body of Jamuri, kidnapper and cutthroat, was discovered on the evening of his murder by a shepherd driving his flock to water at a spring on a hilltop four miles from Gul Tangi Fort. It appeared that the outlaw had been shot at close range from two directions, while in the act of drinking from the pool. It was odd that he had not fallen face-downward into the water, but was lying on his back with his mouth open, as if he had died in the act of savaging an enemy with his teeth. His face had a curiously puffy look, and his grey eyes, which the vultures had not had time to destroy, were wide open. The only living things near him in the immense solitude of the Waziristan hills were a solitary bluebottle which buzzed about his face, and a grey lizard which flickered its tongue at him from a nearby rock.

I happened to be staying at Gul Tangi Fort when news of the assassination came in. There was something about the way Mohammad Zarif modestly averted his eyes when I asked him about Jamuri's death that made me suspect that he had had a hand in it. After a day or so, during which Zarif made no reference to the murder, I questioned him directly. "I have been deeply puzzled," I said, "about the way Jamuri died. As you know," I went on, "several features of the murder make it unlike an ordinary Frontier killing: the fact that there were apparently two assailants – not a lone sniper – who both shot him at close range: the fact that one of the bullets was fired from a service rifle: that Jamuri looked as if he had died in the act of savagely biting something. O Zarif Khan," I ended, "may my inquisitiveness be forgiven, but where were *you* on the afternoon when Jamuri died?"

Zarif Khan answered simply, and without a trace of hesitation, "I was fishing for *mahseer* in the river which skirts the Koh-i-Ashkar, about a mile from where the murder took place. I remember that it was a sunny afternoon and that the fish were not biting, but one fish, and he was the biggest, took the bait – and we killed him." And that was all that Zarif would say on that occasion.

A few days later the Political Agent in charge of the Gul Tangi *'ilaqeh* visited the Fort, and Zarif Khan was summoned to his office. I heard from next door a spate of voluble Pushtu in accusation and explanation, and then the final words spoken in English by the P.A. on a rising note of indignation, "It was nothing but a bloody assassination."

Zarif emerged from the interview looking slightly crestfallen, and soon after was transferred to a distant part of the Frontier. It was there, in Hazara District where I was myself serving, that I learned that Zarif had been transferred from Waziristan in disgrace, though the fact that a Havaldar of the khassadars had accompanied him on the afternoon of Jamuri's murder, and that they had brought back a large *mahseer* as proof of their skill – and of how they had occupied themselves that afternoon – made me wonder how Zarif could be held directly responsible for Jamuri's death.

And yet he was – though I did not learn exactly how until a year later, when Zarif had been restored to favour for his part in the expulsion from the Indus Kohistan of a notorious Mullah, who had been preaching a Jihad, or Holy War. The Gujars, a wonderful people, but simple in their outlook, who every summer drive their flocks up the Kagan Valley to graze around the Safar Maluk Sar Lake, whispered that Zarif had made use of a familiar Djinn to carry the Mullah out of Kohistan, but by then I had come to know Zarif well, and I felt sure that, however modestly he might avert his eyes, it was certainly he who had influenced the Mullah to seek safety in flight, and that it was he also who had been responsible for Jamuri's violent death.

The next time I asked Zarif to tell me the whole story of the murder he spoke as follows: "You must realize, Sahib, that Jamuri was a thoroughly bad man. He was short and stocky, with arms of more than usual length. His chin was fringed by a scraggy beard, and his eyes looked like cold grey stones. The trouble with him was that he had too large a family, and having no land, he found it impossible to feed his children unless he preyed on the fertile valleys of the Settled Area of British territory. He found the most lucrative form of shikar to be Patwaris, and Jamuri made an art of stealing these lowly Government officials, sometimes going as far as twenty miles into British territory in order to capture a victim."

Once Jamuri had selected his prey he would go up to him quietly, and with a pistol protruding from under his voluminous shirt, would silently point the way to the barren hills of Waziristan where he lived. The Patwari was then compelled to walk in front of Jamuri to his village, which was perched on a precipitous spur of the Ashkar Mountains. From there, shortly afterwards, Jamuri would issue a demand for one hundred and fifty rupees, on payment of which the Patwari would be allowed to return home safe and sound.

Mohammad Zarif reluctantly paid for the return of two Patwaris, for the alternative would have been either a costly and certainly useless punitive expedition, or the loss of a highly-trained revenue official. After that Zarif arranged to pay Jamuri, through one of his relatives who was a khassadar serving in Gul Tangi Fort, a monthly allowance of fifteen rupees, in return for which Jamuri agreed to discontinue kidnapping revenue officials of the Government.

This arrangement worked satisfactorily for several months until the mounting pressure of his family needs led Jamuri to ask for the allowance to be raised to twenty-five rupees a month. A few days after this request had been refused another Patwari disappeared, and Jamuri's demand for the payment of two hundred rupees for his safe return was accompanied by a warning that he could not afford to feed the Patwari indefinitely.

It was then that Zarif decided that Jamuri must die. He did not have as much trouble as he had anticipated in finding a suitable assassin. The man he chose was Sa'id Ghulam, the nephew of a certain Mir Alam. Sa'id Ghulam did not possess the usual robust physique of a Wazir, and he was not an outstandingly good shot, but he was young and active, and he bore (though this no one except Zarif seemed to know) a deep grudge against Jamuri. Sa'id Ghulam had hated the outlaw since, two months earlier, he had learned that Jamuri had accepted from an enemy of his uncle an offer of a thousand rupees to kill him. A few days later an unknown sniper fired in the dead of night at Mir Alam who, because of the heat, was sleeping on a charpoy outside his hut on the outskirts of the village. The bullet missed, and Mir Alam gave his would-be murderer no second chance to kill him.

His nephew, Sa'id Ghulam, had no doubt from whose rifle the bullet had been fired, and he at once started to make a plan of revenge. I do not know how far his preparations had advanced when, soon afterwards Zarif, who was always extremely well informed about everything that went on in Tribal Territory, sought him out secretly and suggested that six hundred rupees would be an appropriate reward in the event of Jamuri's life coming to a sudden end during the next few days.

The idea of satisfying family honour, while at the same time winning so rich a prize, appealed strongly to Sa'id Ghulam. The difficulty was how, without raising suspicion, he could lure Jamuri to some lonely spot where he could dispose of him quietly without anyone guessing who had murdered him. It was Zarif who proposed that he himself should be the bait. He was fond of *mahseer* fishing, and often used to fish, protected by outlying picquets of armed khassadars, in the river that runs below Gul Tangi Fort. Sa'id Ghulam, knowing the impasse which had been reached between Zarif and Jamuri over the payment of the latter's allowance, was to suggest to Jamuri that they should go out together to stalk and kill Zarif, who on the selected day would be reported to have gone unprotected (regardless of the danger of such a proceeding) to fish a stretch of the river three miles from the Fort, where he would be an easy target for a rifleman on the heights above the river. Jamuri, having looked with his cold grey eyes searchingly into Sa'id Ghulam's, assented to the proposal, and agreed that Sa'id Ghulam's younger brother, Hajat Khan, should accompany them.

It is impossible to know where the young men planned to kill Jamuri. Perhaps, at the very moment he raised his rifle to fire at Zarif one of the brothers would have leaped on the outlaw and stabbed him to death with the long straight-bladed knife that Wazirs carry. Any preconceived plan was disrupted by the turn the conversation took as they made their way over the hills towards the spot where Zarif, having loaded his second-best rifle and laid it ready on a rock beside him, was preparing his fishing lines.

As they walked along Jamuri, for some reason known to himself, but probably because he was incurably suspicious, turned the conversation to the recent attempt on the life of Mir Alam. At this Hajat Khan, who seems to have been more excitable than his brother, remarked to himself in Jamuri's hearing, that if he ever had the would-be murderer in his power he would stamp his face flat – or words to that affect. The three men were then coming down a gentle slope to a pool of water. It was the hottest hour of the afternoon.

It seems to have been at this moment that a suspicion about his companions' motives began to form in Jamuri's mind, for he suggested that they should stop and drink at the pool. He himself laid his rifle on a rock and squatted down on one side of it, while the two young men, having unslung their rifles, kneeled down about five yards apart, facing him across the water.

When Jamuri had finished drinking he remarked in a casual tone of voice, 'The day has become sultry, my friends. It is now too hot to kill that dog, Zarif. His death at our hands can wait another day,' and, so saying, Jamuri passed his hand over his eyes to wipe away the sweat. As he did so Sa'id Ghulam raised Zarif's Service rifle (which Zarif had sent to him by a secret hand the night before) and fired across the pool at the outlaw.

The bullet passed through Jamuri's chest, but missed his heart. Jamuri was mortally wounded, but he still had sufficient strength to scramble to his feet and run round the pool to grapple with Hajat Khan (who was closer to him than Sa'id Ghulam) shouting, 'You have betrayed me, you Children of the Devil.' On reaching Hajat Khan Jamuri flung his long arms round him, and tried to bite his throat. Hajat gave an anguished shout, 'Brother, kill him or I perish.' Sa'id Ghulam, in order to attack Jamuri from behind, ran swiftly round the pool, and as he did so cried out to Hajat, 'Squeeze thyself away from him, or I cannot fire.' Hajat pressed his hands with all his strength against Jamuri's body, in order to keep him as far away from himself as possible. Sa'id Ghulam then fired at point blank range into Jamuri's right side. This time the bullet passed through his stomach and loin, and Jamuri fell down at Hajat's feet. As he did so he seized hold of one of the young man's legs, and bit it savagely where the tendon joins the heel. Hajat, letting out a scream of pain, swung round and brought his other foot down with all his might on the outlaw's face. Jamuri fell back groaning, the fresh scarlet blood from his wounded lung frothing at the corner of his lips. It was this heavy blow from Hajat's iron-shod *chapli* which caused the peculiar puffiness of the dead man's face, which was so noticeable when the body was found.

Before Jamuri breathed his last he managed to say, 'Sons of Devils, I have sons who will avenge me.' These words sounded like a knell in the ears of the two young men, who still fear the vengeance that Jamuri's descendants may exact. To this day one of Mir Alam's nephews walks the dusty track through Kotkai village with a limp, the reason for which he has never disclosed to anyone except Zarif.

"The rifle shots," Zarif concluded, "which I heard as I drew out of the river the largest *mahseer* I had had the good fortune to catch that summer, were those which killed Jamuri, though I did not learn the full details of how he was killed until the brothers came in for their reward under cover of darkness two days later."

"And I suppose," I said thoughtfully, at the conclusion of the story, "that after Jamuri had been killed, his family slowly starved to death?" "Not while I remained at Gul Tangi Fort, Sahib," he replied, looking downward modestly. "As long as I was there I used to send monthly to his family in Tribal Territory a maund of barley and a maund of wheat. For even the most relentless warfare against the wicked must be tempered with pity for the weak and helpless," said Mohammad Zarif Khan.

Eight

THE DIPLOMACY OF HIGH ASIA

When, long ago at the Resthouse in the shadow of the Fort at Oghi, I started making a written record of these stories, I was intrigued to discover that those tales in which Zarif Khan described his adventures while serving the Raj were no less enthralling than the other stories he told me about people and events with which he had not been personally concerned. This story describes how Mohammad Zarif carried out a difficult assignment for my predecessor as Assistant Commissioner, Mansehra, whom, because he is no longer alive to relish the irony of the tale, I shall simply call Toby O'Brien.

It will be remembered that Mohammad Zarif had been transferred, with a black mark against his name, from Waziristan to the H.Q. of the Mansehra Sub-Division of Hazara District. In making this posting the Chief Secretary of the North-West Frontier Province seems to have borne in mind the character of the Political Officer under whom Zarif would now be serving, for Major O'Brien was well known to be of a choleric and impatient disposition, and what is more, a stern disciplinarian, who (the Chief Secretary must have felt sure) would have no difficulty in curbing Zarif's now known tendency to achieve the aims of Government policy by unorthodox methods of his own invention.

Not long after Zarif's transfer, news reached Mansehra that serious trouble was brewing in the Tribal Territory of the Indus Kohistan, which lies to the west of the upper Kagan Valley. That valley is a tongue of Hazara territory, which curls like a snake round the far side of Kashmir until, at its northern end, it reaches the Chilas border at the summit of the 13,000 foot high Babusar Pass.

The tribes of the Indus Kohistan had been in a state of subdued ferment since the previous summer, when a well-known explorer (who ought to have known better) had insisted on entering and making a prolonged stay in their territory. During the course of his leisurely progress through it a pair of valuable binoculars belonging to him had been stolen, and the efforts my predecessor had made to try to persuade the tribal Maliks to find the binoculars and restore them to their rightful owner had proved unavailing.

The people of the Indus Kohistan were so devoted to the preservation of their lawless independence that they had several times rejected the offers of the Government of India to provide them with schools and a travelling dispensary. Since they regarded the Government's benevolent interest in their welfare as an unwarranted interference in the conduct of their affairs, they cannot be blamed for resenting the explorer's uninvited, and deeply misunderstood, presence among them. Their resentment had been exploited by a fanatical Faqir named Amirah who, early in the summer of Zarif's arrival in Mansehra, had started preaching a Jihad against the British. Amirah's fiery speeches had so influenced some of the hot-headed younger tribesmen that they had laid an ambush for a patrol of the Gilgit Scouts close to the Chilas border, and had succeeded in killing an N.C.O. and wounding three other ranks.

The situation was now full of dangerous possibilities, for retribution would have to be exacted for the attack on the Gilgit patrol, and if this led to an enthusiastic response to the Faqir's call for a Jihad, it would mean that, as soon as the summer was over and the crops harvested, a lashkar of undisciplined riflemen would erupt from the highlands of Kohistan to carry fire and sword into the lowland villages of Hazara. It was therefore of the utmost importance that the Jirga, held each August in the village of Naran in the upper Kagan Valley, to which the Elders of the Kohistani Tribes came to discuss their doubts and difficulties with the Assistant Commissioner, Mansehra, should that summer be an unqualified success.

During July an official letter was sent to the Kohistani Maliks summoning them to meet the Assistant Commissioner at Naran early in August; and a few weeks later Toby O'Brien mounted his sturdy Badakhshani pony and set out on the first march of his seven-day ride up the Kagan Valley from Balakot to Naran. Before leaving Mansehra he bade a tender farewell to his wife, promising that he would be back without fail by the middle of September – in time for the birth of a long-hoped-for son and heir. Mohammad Zarif was meanwhile left in charge at Mansehra to deputize for the absent A.C.

Among the local officials who accompanied O'Brien to Naran was the Mohurrar (the Treasury Clerk of the Sub-Division) who brought with him, packed in a *yakdan* on a led pony, the 3,000 rupees *khercheh*, which the Assistant Commissioner had at his disposal to pay to the Kohistani Tribes. This sum represented a dual resolve on the part of the Government, on the one hand to provide the tribesmen with sufficient cash to meet the basic needs of their austere lives in the mountains of Kohistan, and on the other to guarantee – by the threat of withdrawing the allowance – the continued peaceful behaviour of the Tribes towards their neighbours in Hazara District.

Toby O'Brien must have felt sure that, when it came to the crunch during the forthcoming Jirga, the Tribal Elders would, however reluctantly, agree to accept his advice to expel the Faqir rather than lose the 3,000 rupees he had with him, which they were well aware he had the power either to distribute to them or withhold. As things turned out, Toby was unable to play what he knew to be the trump card in his hand because, on the day appointed for the Jirga to be held in Naran, not one of the Kohistani Maliks put in an appearance.

Toby spent several days fishing for trout in the fast-flowing Kunhar River, while he waited in vain for the tribesmen to appear. Next, he sent a cajoling letter by special messenger across the mountains to Jalkot, and when that elicited no reply, he followed it a few days later with a threatening one. It was to no avail, and at the beginning of September the disappointed and angry Assistant Commissioner, having given up all hope of persuading the Kohistanis to meet him in Naran, mounted his pony, and, followed by his Camp Clerk, Mohurrar, a Naik and Constables of the Indian Police, Chuprassis, servants, and camp followers, jingled off down the Valley towards Balakot.

He was met at Mansehra by Mohammad Zarif who, smiling broadly, expressed his sympathy for the Sahib's discomfiture. 'Oh go to Hell, Zarif,' exclaimed O'Brien, 'or to Naran – if you think you'll be more successful than I.' 'I will go, Sahib, and gladly,' answered Zarif, 'but on condition that, if I am successful in driving Amirah out of our *'ilaqeh*, the black mark against my name will be expunged.' 'I promise,' said the Major, and rode on to greet his wife.

Mohammad Zarif wasted no time. That afternoon he drew from the Treasury 150 rupees, which was the negligible sum sanctioned by the A.C. for him to spend, if necessary, in Naran, and early the following morning he was on his way up the valley from Balakot. By riding double stages he reached Naran by the evening of the third day.

The action Zarif took the next morning spread consternation among the Hindu shopkeepers of Naran. He informed them that they had two days in which to settle their affairs, and that on the third day they would have to accompany him down the valley to Balakot. It was only natural for the *banyas* to raise their voices in protest against this order, but Zarif merely pointed to the Frontier

Constabulary Post at the edge of the village, and asked 'Do you wish to come in fetters?'

That evening the stricken shopkeepers came and prostrated themselves before him. 'Khan Sahib,' they pleaded, 'thou hast always been the Protector of the Poor' (at this Zarif scowled at them and fidgeted with the butt of his revolver), 'give us but *four* days in which to collect our debts from those rascals of Kohistanis, and we will come as thou biddest.' 'Very well,' growled Zarif, 'let them come and settle their accounts with you not later than four days from now – or it will be the worse for you.'

It took no more than a day for the news to spread among the Kohistanis that action was being taken to remove beyond their reach the only shops to which they had access. For the tribesmen this would be disastrous, because from nowhere except Naran could they obtain an essential supply of domestic salt. By such seemingly trivial considerations are the lives of simple people sometimes fundamentally affected!

It is impossible to know how long and how bitter were the arguments which ensued between the Elders, who were determined not to be deprived of salt, and the young hotheads who were equally determined to start a Holy War. What is certain is that, by the evening of the third day, all the tribal Maliks, who had been bidden to the original Jirga and failed to attend it, were now assembled in Naran, ready and anxious to meet Zarif Khan.

The result of the Jirga, held the next morning on a meadow beside the Kunhar River, was inconclusive. Zarif, I am told, addressed the Tribal Elders eloquently in Pushtu (their language and his) for more than two hours, but by the end of the morning he had been able to extract from them nothing more than a written statement to the effect that they would be glad if Amirah left their territory. Their refusal to insist on the Faqir removing himself from the Indus Kohistan was proof that the arguments of the war party had prevailed, and that a Jihad would probably be declared as soon as the crops had been harvested.

It seems likely that Zarif's advocacy would have won acceptance if at that moment he had had available to disburse to the Maliks the 3,000 rupees *khercheh*, which the Assistant Commissioner had brought with him to Naran a month earlier, for, human nature being what it is, a handsome cash payment sometimes proves more convincing than the most eloquent oratory. As it was, Zarif spent half the sum allotted to him on the purchase of two bullocks, which he had slaughtered and their flesh roasted to provide a feast that evening for all who had attended the Jirga. He carefully divided the balance of the money, and paid 15 rupees to each of the leading tribesmen.

It was by no means royal munificence, and yet the extraordinary thing is that when, ten days later, Zarif reported to Major O'Brien in Mansehra, he had what that officer called 'the infernal impudence' to claim that his Kagan mission had achieved complete success. 'What do you mean by saying that?' shouted his enraged superior officer, 'when all you have brought back with you is a dirty bit of paper saying that the Kohistani Elders would be glad if Faqir Amirah moved out of their territory?' 'Have patience, Sahib,' replied Zarif, incling his head modestly, 'for I promise that by the end of next week the Faqir will have fled from our *'ilaqeh*.'

Zarif's prophecy did indeed come true, but *why* it came true Toby O'Brien never guessed. It was sufficient for him to receive, a few days later, a telegram from the Political Agent, Gilgit, which ran, 'Hajji Amirah passed through Gilgit territory into Kashgar night of 16th–17th September. Congratulations.' When Toby had read this message he breathed a sigh of relief and sent for Zarif. Being a generous man, he congratulated him and at once wrote a commendatory letter to the Chief Secretary of the Province, requesting that the remarks entered in Zarif's Confidential File, referring to his 'deplorably unscrupulous methods' should be expunged from the record.

It seems never to have occurred to Toby O'Brien who, with his wife and six-months-old son, was transferred to Baluchistan the following spring, to try to discover by what extraordinary means the threatened Jihad had been averted. But the story of Zarif's successful diplomacy spread up and down the Frontier, and it intrigued me so much that, after I had taken charge of the Mansehra Sub-Division, I several times asked Zarif to tell me the real reason why the Faqir had fled so precipitately from the Indus Kohistan.

It was not till many months later, until in fact the day before I left Mansehra on transfer to the Persian Gulf, that the secret of what had happened was revealed to me. This time Zarif did not shut up like a clam when I asked what miraculous means he had employed in order to get rid of the Faqir. 'It was no miracle, Sahib,' he answered. 'That night in Naran, after I had provided a feast for the Elders of the Tribe, I took a certain Malik aside. I asked him whether it had ever occurred to him to wonder why a British officer as impatient and choleric as Major O'Brien, whose wife moreover might at any moment need him to take her from Mansehra to hospital in Abbottabad for the birth of their child, had remained for nearly a month, *apparently idle*, in Naran. That aroused his interest. 'I know for a fact,' I went on, 'but I would tell no one in the world but thee, that the Sahib has heavily bribed the Jalkotis to assassinate Faqir Amirah before the September moon is half-full.'

'At that moment some of the other Maliks came over from the fire to join us, and he and I had no opportunity for any further conversation. But I know that, within a week, word that the Jalkotis were planning to murder Amirah at the English Sahib's behest had reached him in the depths of Kohistan, and that it was this threat which led him in the middle of September to flee from our territory into Chinese Turkestan. 'Well, Sahib,' concluded Zarif Khan smiling broadly, 'as you know, for me also the story ended happily: Allah be praised for His mercy and compassion.'

Nine

THE STORY OF THE BLIND MAN OF TAXILA

"Today," said Zarif Khan, "I am going to tell you one of the stories that have been handed down from generation to generation, and are still told when families gather round the fire on winter nights in the hill country of Tirah where my boyhood was spent.

"There reigned in Taxila before the coming of Alexander the Great a king named Chandradev, who one day ordered that a sword should be made of such finely-tempered steel that he might be able to sever a man's head from his body at one blow.

"When news of the royal edict became known swordsmiths flocked to Taxila from all over the kingdom, but only one old smith felt capable of accomplishing such a task. He went back to his forge, and after toiling in secret with no one but his wife to work the bellows, he eventually fashioned a sword which seemed to every eye to be of the outstanding excellence required by the king. After its blade had been sharpened to the perfection of a razor's edge and its hilt burnished till it shone like the noonday sun, it was ceremoniously offered to the king in the presence of his courtiers. These all praised the sword, and only one voice, that of an old Blind Man, was raised in criticism of it. 'Let me feel the edge of the blade,' he called, and when the sword was handed to him he held it against his forehead, and declared that its steel would shiver into fragments at the lightest blow. The king's courtiers laughed at the absurdity of this remark, and asked the Blind Man how he could possibly know what would happen when the sword was used. 'The truth can easily be ascertained,' he said, 'if anyone attempts to sever with one blow the stem of a green bullrush.'

"Thereupon the king sent for a bullrush and had it held in front of him. He then took the sword in his hand and tried to sever it, but when the edge of the sword met the fragile green stem it shattered into fragments, and only the chased golden handle of the sword remained in the king's grasp. The Blind Man's prophecy, and the revelation that followed it, impressed the king so favourably that he ordered that he should be given a plate of *dal* and two *chupattis* every day for the remainder of his life.

"A few months later news reached King Chandradev that the ruler of a country to the east of the River Hydaspes was planning to send a mounted expedition against Taxila. In order that his own cavalry, by being sufficiently well mounted, might be able to defeat the threatened invasion, the king sent word to horse-traders throughout the kingdom that on such-and-such a day they must bring their horses to Taxila. When the horses arrived they were collected for inspection on the big open space which served as a parade ground outside the walls of the city. The king then bade his ministers select the horses they considered would be most useful for the coming campaign.

"The ministers, having inspected the horses, chose those that were fat, and rejected those that were lean. The king approved of their choice, but before the matter was concluded the voice of the Blind Man was heard asking if he might give his opinion. The king assented, and the Blind Man walked along the line of horses that had been selected, and as he did so passed his hands over their shoulders and flanks. 'These horses,' he declared, 'are quite unsuitable. Bring me those your ministers have rejected.' The rejected horses were brought, and the Blind Man, having passed his hands over their shoulders and flanks, declared that these were the ones which would be suitable for the king's cavalry. 'If,' he added, 'you require proof that what I say is true, let both the chosen and the rejected horses be driven through the muddy fields below the Deep Ravine (the ravine which is today called the Harro Nullah). When this had been done the wisdom of the Blind Man's choice was proved by the fact that the fat horses all got stuck in the muddy ground, while the lean ones all galloped through it to the other side.

"In the subsequent campaign King Chandradev's cavalry proved its worth by utterly defeating the cavalry sent against it.

"His army's victory so pleased the king that he sent for the Blind Man and asked him how he had known which horses to select. 'O King,' the Blind Man replied, 'I knew that the fat horses had been nourished on buffaloes' milk, and that the lean ones had been nourished on mares' milk, which had made them fleet and strong.' The king was so impressed by the Blind Man's answer that he ordered that a plate of *halwa*, in addition to the *dal* and *chupattis*, should be given to him every day for the rest of his life.

"Not long after this King Chandradev decided to marry the princess of a kingdom beyond the River Indus. When, however, details of the proposed marriage were discussed, the king of that country informed Chandradev that he would not be allowed to set eyes on his daughter before the wedding day. Chandradev, who by now had complete confidence in the Blind Man's sagacity, pleaded that at least the Blind Man should be allowed to touch her forehead. The girl's father refused to agree to this proposal because, he said, it is not our custom for a bride to be touched by any man's hand before her marriage. In the end a compromise was reached, whereby the Blind Man would be allowed to sit on the floor of the pavilion constructed of cedar-wood in the king's garden, while the princess walked across its roof.

"After the Blind Man had listened to the princess walking across the wooden roof above his head, he reported to Chandradev that she would be a suitable wife for him but not for any other king. Chandradev accordingly married her and they spent several weeks of blissful happiness together. The king then recalled the Blind Man's words, and sent for him to enquire why he had told him that the princess would be unfitted to be the wife of any other king. 'For,' said Chandradev, 'I am sure she is the most charming princess in the whole world.'

"The Blind Man replied, 'Unless I am given a promise of complete protection from your wrath, I will not answer your question.' When Chandradev had given his promise the Blind Man said, 'The reason I said she was unfitted to be the wife of any other king is that she is the daughter of a *mirasi*.' These words greatly angered the king, who said, 'How can it have happened that you chose the daughter of a low-caste musician as a suitable wife for me?' 'Because,' replied the Blind Man, 'you yourself are the son of a *banya*.' This reply made Chandradev even more angry, and he shouted at the Blind Man that unless he could prove the truth of his statement he would be guilty of slandering his king. The Blind Man remained quite calm. 'If you want proof of what I have told you,' he said, 'you need only question your mother and your mother-in-law, both of whom will confirm that what I have told you is true.'

"The two ladies were at once sent for and closely questioned by the king. They both admitted the truth of what the Blind Man had said. The king's mother told him, 'I had no son by your father, so there was no heir to the throne. It happened that one summer long ago a handsome young man used to come selling silk *saris* and *phulkari* scarves to the ladies of the palace. One night, when I was sleeping alone upon the palace roof he visited me, and it is he who is your father.'

"The king was utterly amazed by his mother's story, and next questioned his mother-in-law, who said, 'During the hot summer evenings long ago my husband and I used to have a young *mirasi* to play his *sitar* to help lull us to sleep. One night, when I was unable to fall asleep, I slipped out and dallied with the young musician, and it is he who is the father of my daughter, the princess.'

"This story likewise astonished and dismayed the king, who then asked the Blind Man how he could possibly have guessed the secret of the paternity of his bride. The Blind Man answered, 'When I listened to the princess making her way across the roof, I noticed that she did not walk calmly and modestly as a princess might be expected to walk. Instead she crossed it with light rhythmic steps, as if she could hear music to which her feet were keeping time. I therefore concluded that she was a musician's daughter, and of lowly origin.'

"The king then said to the Blind Man, 'I have no option but to believe that what these ladies have said is true, but what I still cannot understand is what led you to deduce that my father was a *banya*.' 'That question is easily answered,' said the Blind Man. 'On the first occasion, when I was able to demonstrate to you the true quality of the swordblade that had been so zealously fashioned for you, you favoured me with a miserly allowance of a plate of pulse and a modicum of bread. On the second occasion when, by choosing the best horses for your cavalry, I saved your kingdom from destruction, you were gracious enough to add a plate of pudding to my daily allowance of food. It was obvious to me that such meanness betokened the narrow outlook of a tradesman, rather than the generous character of a king.' "For," concluded Zarif, "as the poet Firdausi wrote in the margin of his great *Shah Nameh* after he had presented it to Sultan Mahmud,

If the king had been of royal blood
He would have placed a crown of gold upon my head."

Ten

THE CONUNDRUM OF THE THREE SUITORS OF THE PRINCESS OF BAGHDAD

"As far as I can remember," said Zarif Khan one winter evening, when we had finished our work and were sitting in front of a bright fire of mulberry logs in the Resthouse below the walls of Oghi Fort, "I have never related to you the tale which my grandfather's friend Emran told when he wanted to confound the Mullah of the village where he lived.

"I am sure you know," went on Mohammad Zarif, "that our Mullahs, like the priests of other religions, tend to regard themselves as infallible, and certainly the Mullah of Nassian village used to boast that he had never been proved wrong in any argument in which he had been involved, and had never failed to answer correctly any conundrum that had ever been put to him. The story that I am going to tell you, is the one related by Emran with the intention of putting an unanswerable conundrum to the Mullah of Nassian."

* * *

"There reigned long ago in Baghdad a Caliph who had a beautiful daughter, whom he greatly cherished. One morning when she was seated beside him, and he was caressing her long dark hair, which was as full of waves as the River Hydaspes when it flows forth from the mountains, she suddenly burst into tears. 'Light of my Life,' exclaimed the Caliph, 'dry thy tears, and tell me what is the matter.' The Princess answered, 'You are loving and generous to me now while I am still a child, but I am afraid that in a little while you will marry me to some elderly Prince, and that the spring and summer of my life will be spent in tears and lamentation, instead of, as it ought to be, in the enjoyment of love with some brave and solicitous young man.'

"The Caliph then swore a great oath that the Princess should marry whomsoever she wished, and although she was his only daughter, and therefore a valuable counter in the game of diplomacy which it was his duty and pleasure to play, he at once sent for the Grand Vizier and ordered him to tear up the Draft Proposal for a Dynastic Marriage between the Princess Zulaika (for that was her name) and the Prince of Marv, who was indeed a powerful potentate, but far older than the Princess and as empty of tender feelings as a cockle shell.

"The Caliph then ordered a *Firman* to be proclaimed in Baghdad and throughout the whole of Mesopotamia, Arabia, Persia, and the provinces of Asia Minor bordering the Empire of Rum, which stated simply, 'Know by these Presents [for such is the language in which Royal Proclamations have to be couched] that WHOSOEVER wishes will be permitted to wed the Daughter of the Shadow of God on Earth, Her Highness the Princess Zulaika.'

"Then, secure in the knowledge that he had kept his word, and in the belief that he had done as his daughter the Princess desired, the Caliph retired to the seclusion of the white marble *Baradari* at the centre of the Garden of Morning Calm, intending to devote the remainder of the day to contemplating the subtle colours, to studying the intricate design, and to counting the almost invisible stitches of a carpet which had that day reached him as a gift from the Governor of the distant Persian province of Isfahan.

"The Caliph's meditation was brought to an abrupt conclusion by the arrival of the Princess who, running lightly up the marble steps, entered the *Baradari* and angrily confronted her father. She was looking more beautiful than ever, with her dark hair caught in a golden fillet, and her face flushed with vexation. 'Father,' she cried, 'that was not at all a good plan of yours.' 'But my child . . .' began the old man. 'No, no, *no*,' cried the Princess stamping her small foot in rage. 'You have made us both look ridiculous. A vast concourse has gathered outside the Palace, and when the Commander of the Guard shouts abuse at them and orders them to disperse they refuse to go home, claiming that they have come to demand my hand in marriage. A number of the most scaly beggars of Baghdad are there, together with every sort of merchant and shopkeeper, and, Oh Father, such a lot of horrid old men. Please, *please*, Father, order them to go away; and then try to think of some other more sensible plan.'

"The Caliph breathed a deep sigh, and then, putting on his shoes and turban, made his way slowly to the entrance to the Palace. The gate which guarded it was pierced by a small grille to enable those within to converse with those outside, and through this aperture the Caliph saw that, the hour being almost noon and the day extremely hot, the men of every age, shape, and size, who had come to claim the Princess's hand, were falling into a mood of bewildered frustration that might at any moment lead to violence and bloodshed. He therefore addressed them in a very conciliatory tone of voice – praising them one and all for their sincere admiration (to which their presence bore witness) for his dear daughter, the Lady Zulaika, and regretting that so many distinguished persons of brilliant intellect should have completely misunderstood the purport of the Proclamation – with the result that (as he took care to point out) they were now needlessly standing in front of the Palace at the uncomfortably hot hour of noon.

"The Caliph went on to suggest that they could not have listened carefully to the Proclamation which, he said, had made it clear that only young men might apply, and only those young men who could bring with them a Marvel such as had never been seen in the world before. In this way the Caliph hoped to be rid of the whole vexatious affair. Since most of those who had gathered in front of the Palace had heard, in the hubbub of the Bazaar, only the tail-end of the Proclamation, or had idly listened to it while sipping tea in one of the *cha'i-khanehs* of the town, they accepted the Caliph's words as being the truth of the matter, and murmuring to each other, 'There was bound to be a catch in it somewhere,' departed each one to his own house."

* * *

"There were living in Baghdad at that time three young men, who had completed their military service in the army of the Caliph, each of whom was looking round for a wife to keep him in comfort for the rest of his days. They were all three very conceited, and were considered an intolerable nuisance by the shopkeepers of the ward in which they lived, for they were forever up to some trick or another, and their impudence was only equalled by their contempt for people who earned their living in an honest fashion.

It came to the ears of these three young men, whose names were Yakub, Ishaq and Yasin, that whosoever wished to win the Princess's hand must present himself at the Palace the next morning, bringing with him some extraordinary Marvel. 'Is not the sword-cut wound in my thigh sufficient marvel for any right-minded girl?' asked Yakub. 'And the way I can in a matter of minutes make a dwarf pomegranate tree put on leaves and blossom?' (for that is a trick he had learned recently in the Thieves' Bazaar) said Ishaq. 'Or the back-somersault that those devils of Kazzaks taught me?' said Yasin, who had recently returned from campaigning in the North. 'Of a truth,' exclaimed Yakub, 'if the Princess has seen any such marvels – and she has not yet seen my wound – she is certainly better instructed than we had thought.' They accordingly decided to present themselves at the Palace early the following day as suitors for the Caliph's daughter's hand.

"The next morning each young man dressed himself with elaborate care in clothes as gorgeous as the occasion demanded. Yakub had oiled and curled his moustaches till they gleamed like moonbeams on the Tigris; Ishaq was wearing a turban of the finest silk in shades of turquoise, amethyst, and ultramarine; while into Yasin's cummerbund was thrust a dagger, the handle of which was encrusted with rosy gems.

"Yakub's moustaches were indeed his own, though their smooth sweep was due to the attention paid to them during a visit early that morning to a nearby *hammam*. On the other hand the yards of brightly-coloured silk, which formed the folds of Ishaq's turban had been part of a bale of silk that had slipped unnoticed in the dark from a tired camel just before it reached the Caravan Serai within the city's Eastern Gate. It was known to his friends that, before the loss of the bale was discovered, Ishaq had taken the opportunity to extract from it this very turban-length of shining silk. Yasin's jewelled dagger had come into his possession no less fortuitously after he had been appointed orderly to the commander of a *toman* of the Caliph's cavalry, who had shortly afterwards been killed in a brush with a party of Turkoman raiders. Yasin, who had been left behind on the battlefield to succour the wounded, waited only long enough to see his master's eyes closed in death, before extracting from his belt, and purloining the jewelled dagger on which he had already cast envious eyes.

"Because the Caliph had, on the previous day, himself intervened to help solve the problem of finding a suitable bridegroom for his daughter, Yakub had foreseen considerable difficulty in obtaining permission for himself and his fellow-suitors to enter the closely-guarded walls of the Palace. He had therefore armed himself with a roll of parchment, embossed with the royal seal (for he had a friend in one of the offices of the Government), on which he had inscribed a verse from the Koran in jet-black ink in an elaborate style of writing. This document Yakub presented with a flourish to the sentry on duty at a side gate of the royal residence. The sentry studied it carefully for several minutes, holding it upside down (for he had no notion how to read) before handing it back without making any comment. He then unlocked the gate and allowed Yakub and his friends to enter the Palace.

"They found themselves in a paved passage, along which they made their way. It ended in a graceful arch through which could be seen an expanse of green grass, intersected by a narrow water-course and bordered by a mass of wild Persian roses. The windows of Zulaika's bedroom looked on to this quiet cypress-shadowed demesne.

"It happened that, at the moment the three young men entered her garden, Zulaika, who had just worken from a dreamless sleep, was standing at the open window. To her surprise she heard herself addressed – once, twice, and again:

'O *Star the unclouded morning wears upon her brow*,' cried Yakub, bowing so low that his moustaches swept the grass;

'O *Dewdrop from a Persian rosebud's heart*,' cried Ishaq, making so splendid an obeisance that, if his turban had not been firmly tied, it would certainly have fallen from his head;

'O *Moon that bids the shining planets pale*,' cried Yasin, prostrating himself with such violent enthusiasm that the jewelled hilt of his dagger drove sharply into his stomach.

'O *Pearl so perfect that a diver must forever search for it in vain*,' they called out in unison, addding as the clamour grew, 'We have come to claim your hand . . .' 'I can do such-and-such . . .' 'My wound . . .' 'My pomegranate . . .' 'My somersault . . .' *My word what a noise!*

"Their voices soon grew to such a babel that the Princess had to press her fingers to her ears and beg them to stop. By then Yasin was performing a series of back-somersaults which were rapidly taking him to the other end of the garden, while Ishaq had produced from under a scarf he had brought with him a grove of dwarf pomegranate trees, which were already bursting into bloom. Yakub was still standing below her window with a perplexed look on his face. He was wondering whether his sword-cut wound, though undeniably more diverting than such stale tricks, would after all prove of life-and-death interest to the Caliph's daughter.

"As Yakub appeared at that moment to be the only one of the three who had not completely taken leave of his senses, Zulaika begged him to tell her the reason for their visit. So, while Ishaq added a further row to his pomegranate plantation, and Yasin disappeared backwards over a hedge, Yakub told her how they had come to hear about the Royal Decree that only such young men as could bring with them a particular marvel might present themselves as suitors for her hand. He added that, having heard of her great beauty – though nothing that had come to their ears could compare with the evidence of their eyes – they had found their way into the Palace in order to show the Princess what each of them could do, in the fervent hope of winning her hand.

"The Princess did not ask Yakub what he himself had to show her, for she had an idea that it might be something not quite nice. Instead she shook her head and said, 'I'm afraid my father, the Caliph, meant real marvels, such as Unicorns, Winged Dragons, or Hyrcanian Tigers, and it would never do, now that the new *Firman* has been proclaimed, for me to accept just ordinary tricks, like those your friends have been showing me.'

"On hearing Zulaika's unkind words Ishaq stood up from his planting and stared at her incredulously while Yasin, who had reappeared somewhat out of breath from his exertions, gave her a very cross look. Then, as the three young men stood before her open window, abashed by her criticism but still enchanted by her beauty, she pronounced their doom. And this is what she said: 'O Princelings of Baghdad [by addressing them thus she hoped to salve their self-esteem, for they had succeeded in making themselves more than a little ridiculous] you have dared where no one else has even tried, and I will marry that one of the three of you who brings me the greatest marvel either to see, or to touch, or to smell.' And being a practical girl she added, 'Be sure that it is something useful.'

"The Princess could not help noticing how at these words the faces of the young men fell, so, bending towards them over the window-sill, she added in a whisper, 'My old nurse says that in a house behind the Coppersmiths' Bazaar there lives a Magician who has a knowledge of truly great marvels.' She then closed the window and, with a wave of her hand, bade farewell to her accepted suitors – for such they now were."

* * *

"The sun was setting that evening when Yakub knocked softly on the door of a shuttered house in a lane behind the Coppersmiths' Bazaar. The door was opened by the Magician himself – an old man with a long white beard, who peered at him keenly through pebble glasses. He led Yakub into a vaulted chamber, with a brazier glowing in the middle of it, beside which a black cat sat purring softly. He then climbed on to a high stool and bade Yakub tell him the nature of his business.

"When Yakub had finished relating the circumstances of his courtship of the Caliph's daughter, the Magician pronounced an incantation, and threw a handful of aromatic herbs on to the brazier, making it blaze up suddenly, so that the darkened chamber seemed momentarily filled with leaping djinns. It had the effect of waking the cat, which at once jumped on to Yakub's lap, startling him considerably.

"The Magician then said, 'I can indeed help you achieve your ambition, but your journey will be full of hardship and will take you many months to accomplish.' He went on to describe in a low monotonous voice a Globe of Pure Crystal in which, if a man gazed and revolved it seven times seven with his thoughts centred on the object of his desire, he would be able to see all that he wished, though it might be half the world away. 'This Magic

Globe,' he said, 'lies hidden in a cave in the mountains seven marches east of the Gate of Jade, through which the great caravans of the Silk Road make their way into China. See that you bring this marvel to me after you have persuaded the Princess. Now go, for your way is long and arduous.

"Yakub bowed low to the Magician and thanked him sincerely for his kindness. Then, being careful to avoid kicking the cat as he went out, he left the shuttered house behind the Coppersmiths' Bazaar, and soon after set out on his travels.

"A little later Ishaq, who had found his way to the same house, knocked on the door, and was ushered inside. 'There is no need for you to tell me the nature of your business,' said the Magician, 'for I know why you have come. You shall find what you desire, but your journey will be full of hardship, and will take many months to accomplish.'

"The Magician paused, and bending from his high stool to trace on Ishaq's forehead a sign of the Zodiac at the very moment when the young man was stooping to stroke the cat (for he was fond of animals) the Magician overbalanced and fell headlong on top of his visitor and his cat, almost consigning both of them to fiery immolation in the brazier, which gleamed, and glowed, and sparkled in the darkness of the vaulted room.

"The Magician went on to describe, in a low monotonous voice, how in a shop without a name in a *kucheh* leading nowhere, behind the Great Mosque in Bukhara, Ishaq might be able to find a carpet of undistinguished colour but of rare design, on which if he seated himself cross-legged, facing in the direction of the Shrine in the Holy City of Mashad, and repeated a certain magic word (which the Magician confided to him) he would be able to fly wheresoever he wished, though it might be half the world away. 'Be sure,' said the Magician, 'to bring this marvel to me when you have persuaded the Princess. Now go, for among all the carpets in the city of Bukhara you must make long and diligent search.'

"Ishaq bowed low to the Magician and thanked him sincerely

for his kindness. Then, being careful to avoid letting the cat out on to the street (for the animal had taken a great fancy to him) Ishaq left the shuttered house behind the Coppersmiths' Bazaar, and soon after set out on his travels.

"A little later Yasin, who had belatedly decided to visit the house with the closed shutters, found his way to its door and knocked gently. 'Confound these lovesick boys,' exclaimed the Magician, 'but anyway this is the last of them,' and, so saying, he bent down and poured out for his cat a stiff nightcap of milk punch (for the night had grown chilly). As Yasin entered the vaulted chamber he could not help noticing that the Magician was in the act of replacing on an upper shelf, among a score of medicine bottles, one clearly marked 'Magic Potion No. 1. To be taken mixed with only a very little milk.'

"'I know why you have come,' said the Magician, 'and you shall achieve what you desire, but the journey will be long and arduous.' Then, while the brazier threw up golden sparks into the vaulted darkness, during a silence broken only by a loud hiccough from the cat (which had found the mixture that evening rather rich) the magician started to describe in a low monotonous voice how in a green valley below the Pir Panjal range in the very centre of Kashmir a cedar, found growing nowhere else in the world, weeps its medicinal gum into a pool of pure water fed by a spring far up the mountainside.

"'Of the resin,' the Magician went on, 'you must collect a sufficient quantity as will, when compacted, fill this container (and here the Magician took from a pocket in his black gown a little silver box which he placed in Yasin's hand. Seal it with wax by means of this taper, and carry it with you by night and by day wherever you go, until such time as it is needed to cure someone who is mortally ill. Then, and then only, open the box, pronouncing as you do so the magic word (which I will now confide to you) and allow the bitter-sweet resinous scent to mingle with the patient's breath. From that moment complete recovery will start.

Go now, for you have a long and hazardous journey before you. And be sure,' added the Magicain, 'to bring back to me the silver box when you have persuaded the Princess.'

"Yasin thanked the Magician sincerely for his kindness, and having laid the black cat (which had gone off into an intoxicated slumber) carefully on the Magician's truckle bed, he bowed low, and left the house, and soon after set out on his travels."

* * *

"Many months later Yakub reached the Holy City of Mashad on his way back to Baghdad. He had succeeded in finding and carrying away with him from the cave in the mountains seven marches east of the Gate of Jade, the Globe of Pure Crystal which the Magician had described to him. He had arrived that evening at the Caravan Serai on the outskirts of the city, and was waiting for his mules (one of which carried the precious Crystal Globe) to be unloaded when, to his surprise, he saw Ishaq come through the archway into the Serai.

"The two friends had not met since the morning when they had foregathered in the garden below Princess Zulaika's window to claim her hand. They at once fell into conversation, each pretending that he had undertaken a long and perilous journey in order to forget the disappointment of his rejected suit, rather (said Zarif) in the way young Englishmen during the early years of this century, used to go off and shoot lions in Africa in the belief that discomfort and danger might help to heal their lacerated hearts.

"Yakub and Ishaq had no sooner sat down to refresh themselves with bowls of green tea in a *cha'i-khaneh* close to the entrance to the Serai, than Yasin walked in and sat down beside them. He had no difficulty in adding to the stories of their adventures which were being told by his friends, for, after overcoming great difficulties, he had found his way to the green valley below the Pir Panjal range, and had succeeded in collecting a sufficient quantity of the

Medicinal Gum to fill the silver box entrusted to him by the Magician.

"After supper, which the three friends ate wrapped in their *poshteens* under the bright winter stars, the talk turned to the evil state of the roads, the rapaciousness of the muleteers, and the poor quality of the baggage animals provided by them. Noticing that Ishaq had fallen silent, Yakub turned to him and said, 'Ishaq, has not that been your experience also in the lands where you have been travelling?' Ishaq who, since meeting his friends unexpectedly in Mashad, had been longing to reveal to them the manner in which he had reached there, replied a little contemptuously, 'To tell you the truth I do not know, for I came here flying on a carpet. Yes,' he added, 'look not so amazed. After I had searched in Bukhara for many weary weeks, I at last found the carpet I was looking for, as indeed a friend of mine in Baghdad ('Ah ha,' murmured Yakub and Yasin, for they guessed who that friend was) foretold that I would. This afternoon, having paid only a reasonable sum, for the rug is old and shabby, and its owner knew nothing of its magical qualities, I took it to the great *Maidan* at the city's centre, and sat cross-legged upon it. Then, after I had spoken a magic word which had been confided to me, I arrived here in the twinkling of an eye.'

"When Ishaq's friends heard the story of his successful search for the Magic Carpet they were utterly astonished, though they pretended not to be, lest their expression of even a modicum of surprised congratulation might unduly enhance the value of the carpet in its new owner's eyes. Not to be outdone, Yakub related how he had brought back from a cave in the mountains east of the Gate of Jade a Crystal Globe which would enable him to see what he desired, though it might be half the world away. Finally it was the turn of Yasin to describe the Medicinal Gum, which he had collected from a pool in the green centre of Kashmir.

"An argument ensued among the three young men as to which of the marvels they were bringing back with them to offer to the

Princess was in fact the most marvellous. 'Mine,' declared Yakub, 'is certainly the most useful to us at this moment, for by its means we can look at the object of our adoration, the Princess Zulaika, whose beauty has for so many months been hidden from our eyes.'

"On his friends agreeing to this proposal, Yakub went and fetched the saddlebag in which the Crystal Globe had travelled with him from China. He unwrapped it, and setting it down in front of them, revolved it (as the Magician had instructed him) seven times seven with his thoughts concentrated on the Princess. At first, as the young men bent over the globe, they could see nothing but a pool of swirling milk-white vapour, behind which a bright light shone. The next moment the mist cleared from the heart of the crystal, and they found themselves looking into Zulaika's bedroom in the Palace at Baghdad.

"There they beheld the Princess lying on her bed, not warm and joyous as when they had last seen her, but looking pale and exhausted, with a mortal fever on her brow. The Caliph was kneeling at her bedside murmuring words of tender solicitude, which the poor Princess seemed hardly able to comprehend.

"'There is only one thing to be done,' cried Ishaq, 'we must jump on my magic carpet and fly this minute to Baghdad.' 'And as soon as we have reached there,' chimed in Yasin, 'I shall with my marvellous resin bring the Princess back to life.' The three friends at once sat cross-legged on the carpet, the magic word was spoken, and they were instantly transported to Baghdad.

"A moment or so after Yasin had given Zulaika the magic balm to breathe, the colour started flooding back into her cheeks, and to her father's amazement she sat up in bed, and drawing a wrap round her shoulders, held out her hands to the three young men. 'Dear, dear friends,' she said, 'how can I thank *all three of you* enough?'"

Here Zarif broke off and said, "That is as far as the story goes. The question the Mullah of Nassian was called on to answer was which of the three suitors Zulaika decided to marry. The Princess had said that she would accept the suitor who succeeded in bring her the greatest marvel, and she had added that it must be something useful. As things turned out, she must have realized that if the young men had not been able to use Yakub's crystal globe to look from a great distance, they could not have known that she was mortally ill; if they had not been able to use Ishaq's magic carpet they could not have arrived in time; and, if Yasin's miraculous gum had not been available to effect an immediate cure, her life could not have been saved.

"What," asked Zarif Khan, "do *you* think she decided?" "I am," I confessed, "as perplexed as the Mullah must have been, but," I said, "I suppose the Princess had in fact, during the intervening period, married some eminently suitable bachelor nearer home." "She had not," replied Zarif, "for she had given her word that she would marry one of the three friends. And indeed she might just as well have married one as either of the other two – for they were all three great rascals."

Glossary

'Ala Hazrat	(Persian). Your Majesty.
Arg	Citadel.
Badmash	A rogue. A man of criminal character.
Banya	A Hindu shopkeeper.
Bāradari	A garden-pavilion. (This Persian word means literally 'a building with 12 doors'.)
Chādur	A sheet or blanket.
Chā'i-khāneh	A tea-house.
Chapli	A stout leather sandal.
Chārpoy	A wooden-framed bed, with a surface of webbing or hempen rope. (From the Persian, *chahār pā'i*, meaning 'something with four feet'.)
Chenār	The Oriental Plane tree. The most beautiful and venerable *chenārs* in the whole of Afghanistan are those planted by the first Mogul Emperor, Babur (A.D. 1483–1530), on a hilltop close to the village of Istalif, some 40 miles N.E. of Kabul.
Chupatti	*The Shorter Oxford English Dictionary* describes a chupatti as 'a small cake of unleavened bread, of coarse wheaten meal, flattened, and baked on a griddle'.
Chuprassi	An office Orderly or Messenger. (From the Hindi word 'chapras', the official badge worn by him.)
Dāl	Cooked lentils.
Durāni	The Durāni tribes inhabit the area of western Afghanistan which, before the destruction of the Persian Empire by Ghengiz Khan in the thirteenth century A.D. formed part of its great eastern province of Khurasan. As a result, they are deeply imbued with Persian culture, and speak a form of Persian known as 'Dāri'. From the emergence of Afghanistan as a country in the middle of the eighteenth century until modern times, the Ruling House has been consistently Durāni, and it is quite true that Warburton's mother was a Durāni Princess, for she was a niece of the Emir Dōst Mohammad Khān.
Durbār	A public audience or levee, held by the Ruler of a country, or his representative.

Faqīr	A Hindu or Muslim ascetic: a religious mendicant.
Firmān	A Royal or Imperial Edict.
Ghulāmbacheh	A palace-servant. (The literal meaning of this Persian word is 'slave-child'.)
Gūjar	A race of cattlemen, widespread in north-western India and Pakistan, some of whom migrate annually to their summer grazing-grounds in the upper Kāgān Valley.
Halwa	An Indian sweetmeat.
Hammām	An old-fashioned, but comparatively luxurious bath-house, built over a wood-burning furnace, such as to this day provides comfort for travellers by road in the rural areas of Turkey and Persia.
Havaldār	An infantry sergeant. (From the Persian, meaning 'one who holds charge'.)
Hazāra	The most northerly Administrative District of the North-West Frontier Province of what used to be India, and is now Pakistan.
Hydaspes	The Greek name, dating from the invasion of India by Alexander the Great in 327 B.C., of the River Jhelum, which is one of the five great rivers which have given the Punjab its name.
'Id	A Muslim religious festival.
'Ilāqeh	An administrative area, zone, or domain.
Jāgīr	A revenue-free assignment of land.
Jālkōtis	A sub-section of the leading Kohistāni tribe.
Jemadār	*The Shorter Oxford English Dictionary* explains this word as 'a native officer in a Sepoy regiment, corresponding to a lieutenant; also a name for the head of a body of Police, etc., or of servants'.

The original significance of the Urdu word *jam'a* was 'collection', and when, on joining the Indian Political Service in November 1934 I was appointed Personal Assistant to the Resident at Hyderabād, I could not help being diverted by the fact that the Court of His Exalted Highness the Nizām of Hyderabād was adorned by no less a personage than the Shaikh (the Emir) of Mukalla (on the coast of Arabia N.E. of Aden) who, in his own country had the status of nine-gun-salute Prince, but, because he was Jemadār to the Nizām, that is to say the recruiter of his own subjects as troops for H.E.H's Regiment of Arabian Cavalry, was held in low esteem in Hyderabād State.

I got to know His Highness of Mukalla quite well because we both – I as A.D.C. to the Resident, and he as a mere collector of recruits – used to be assigned the two bottom places at the end of the table at each of the huge luncheons which used to be given by Sālār Jung and the other great nobles of Hyderabād State in the days when H.E.H. the Nizām was still in every sense, as his official designation described him, 'The Faithful Ally of the British Government'. Alas, long since no more . . .

Jihād	A Mohammedan Holy War against unbelievers.
Jirga	A consultative or judicial conference of Tribal Elders.
Khassadār	A locally-recruited militiaman, employed to help maintain security in the tribal areas bordering Afghanistan.
Khercheh	Expenses.
Kōh	(Persian *kūh*). A mountain. *Safēd Kōh* is the 'White (or snow-covered) Mountain'.
Kūcheh	(Persian). A lane.
Lashkar	A tribal army, or raiding force.
Mahseer	The Indian Carp. A fresh-water sporting fish, which sometimes runs to a very great size.
Maidān	A Persian word meaning an open space or parade ground, in or near a town.
Malik	A Persian word meaning a 'lord' or chief', but used in this book in the sense, customary in Afghanistan and the North-West Frontier, of a 'Tribal Elder'.
Mansehra	Mansehra is the name of the town which, when I took over as Assistant Commissioner in the autumn of 1943, was the H.Q. of the Sub-Division of that name. (It has subsequently been raised to the status of a District.) In those days it comprised the whole of the north-eastern area of Hazara District, which itself, including Feudal Tanawal, covered an area of more than 3,000 square miles, and extended from near Taxila in the south to Chilas in the north; and from the River Indus in the west to the borders of Poonch and Kashmir on the east. It was not an unusually responsible or exacting assignment for a man of my age (I was then thirty-four) or experience, but it looked like being an enthralling one. As, indeed, it proved to be!
Māntra	A Sanskrit word meaning 'instrument of thought'. Māntras are texts from the Hindu Scriptures, used as prayers or incantations.
Maund	A maund weighs 80 lb. The word itself is an anglicized form of the Persian and Urdu word *man* which has a venerable ancestry, for it is believed to be of Chaldean origin.
Mirāsi	A wandering musician.

Mohurrar	A clerk or archivist.
Naik	A corporal
Oghi	A village in the Agror Valley 20 miles N.W. of Mansehra. Because it lies close to the line of demaraction between Hazara District and Feudal Tanawal on the one side and the Black Mountain Tribal Territory (the scene of much bitter fighting during the nineteenth century) on the other, it is guarded by a Fort garrisoned by the Frontier Constabulary.
Patwāri	A Government revenue official, one of whose duties is to measure each cultivated field for purposes of assessment.
Phūlkāri	A Persian word meaning 'flower-work'. A *phūlkāri* scarf is one embroidered with flowers.
Pilau	A savoury oriental dish of boiled rice and meat, garnished with almonds and raisins.
Shamiāna	A tented pavilion.
Sipah Sālār	(Persian). A general.
Sitār	An oriental stringed musical instrument.
Sūbahdār	This Persian word, meaning 'one who holds charge of a province', was originally used to designate the Governor of a Province of the Mōgul Empire. It is today the rank of a senior non-commissioned officer in an Indian or Pakistani Infantry regiment.
Poshteen	An ankle-length greatcoat of reversed goat or sheepskin, decorated with simple chain-stitch designs, worn by men during the winter on the Afghan border.
Sādhu	One who has renounced materialism in order to attain the Buddhist Nirvana, which is the extinction of all desires and passions and the attainment of perfect beatitude.
Sangar	A stone fortification.
Sudbāshi	(Persian). The commander of a hundred men.
Tomān	A Persian word now meaning a sum of ten Rials, but used in former times to designate a small military formation such as, in this case, a troop of cavalry.
Vaisya	In the Hindu caste system the Vaisya (Mercantile) caste ranks third after the Brāhman (Priestly) and Kashtriya (Warrior) castes.
Yakdān	A light, stout, rectangular leather box, designed to be carried conveniently on a yak. A 'must' for anyone planning a journey through Central Asia!